# ROOM 553

BRITNEY KING

WWW.BRITNEYKING.COM

# ALSO BY BRITNEY KING

*HER*

*Speak of the Devil*

*The Replacement Wife*

*The Social Affair*

*Water Under The Bridge*

*Dead In The Water*

*Come Hell or High Water*

*Bedrock*

*Breaking Bedrock*

*Beyond Bedrock*

*Around The Bend*

*Somewhere With You*

*Anywhere With You*

# ROOM 553

BRITNEY KING

# COPYRIGHT

ROOM 553 is a work of fiction. Names, characters, places, images, and incidents are products of the author's imagination or are used fictitiously and are not to be construed as real. Any resemblance to actual events, locales, organizations, persons, living or dead, is entirely coincidental and not intended by the author. The scanning, uploading, and distribution of this book without permission is a theft of the author's intellectual property. No part of this publication may be used, shared or reproduced in any manner whatsoever without written permission except in the case of brief quotations embodied in critical articles and reviews. If you would like permission to use material from the book (other than for review purposes), please contact http:// britneyking.com/contact/

Thank you for your support of the author's rights.

*For Monica, who makes random women appear. You're better than superwoman.*

"The most common lie is that which one lies to himself; lying to others is relatively an exception." – Friedrich Nietzsche

# FOREWORD

Take my advice, if you're reading this: Quit while you're ahead. Put it down. Walk away. A few chapters in and you'll wish you had. It won't be long now. Save yourself. It's not too late. Get out while you can.

Surely, there is something better you could be doing. Why bother with this? You could just as easily be scrolling social media. Netflix and binge, or *Netflix and chill*—whatever the cool kids are calling it these days—you could do that. Treat yourself to a latte. Call your mom. Mow your lawn. Take one of those master classes on the internet. You know, the ones taught by celebrities? I hear they're good.

You could make something out of yourself.

It's not like you're getting any younger.

What happens here is just going to piss you off. Trust me, it only goes downhill from there.

Really. If you can do anything else, do that.

This is not a joke. It's not some reverse psychology gimmick. What you're getting is a terrible story about a highly educated, very stupid man. A terrible, pretty much true-life story about people you'd never want to meet. If you decide to continue on, do so at your own risk.

But don't say I didn't warn you.

# PROLOGUE

A *DO NOT DISTURB* tag hangs on the door. The watch on Carol Mesa's wrist reads one p.m. The fifth floor of the Belmond Hotel has nearly emptied. Checkout was at eleven, and Carol's roster does not show the guest in the presidential suite as having late checkout.

More than likely, the tag was an oversight, just a missed detail on the way out the door. Carol decides to call down to the front desk, just to be sure. Guests don't appreciate being caught off guard, and she isn't particularly fond of it either. After twenty years in hospitality, few things still surprise her, but this isn't the point. One complaint to management can lower her star rating, and Carol prides herself on quality.

Once, twice, three raps. She knocks at the door. "Housekeeping."

Carol listens for signs of life in the room. She waits. She looks for the shifting of light, searches for movement beneath the door. Carol sees nothing, hears nothing. At her feet, the complimentary newspaper has been left untouched, serving as further confirmation that its occupant was likely in a hurry to exit and simply forgot to remove the door tag.

9

She takes a deep breath in and lets it out. Everyone is in a hurry these days, Carol included. She checks her watch, her roster, and then phones the front desk once more. As it is, she doesn't have much time to put the remaining rooms in shape before the influx of new guests arrive in a few hours. This is why, on the fifth ring, she hangs up and makes the decision to leave the suite for last.

At approximately one-thirty, she calls down to the front desk again. Management is adamant that hospitality report guests who straggle, this way they can charge them. On the third ring, an unfamiliar voice picks up. The trainee assures Carol the room should be empty.

Once again, she knocks on the door. She calls out, "House-keeping," according to protocol.

When no response comes, she grabs cleaning supplies from her cart, swipes her fob across the reader on the door, and enters the suite. At first glance, Room 553 is like any of the other dozen rooms she's serviced already: dark, stuffy, and unkempt.

It isn't until she's halfway into the living area of the suite, as she moves to open the curtains, that a shadow causes her to stop in her tracks.

When she jerks back, Carol realizes the shadow is her own. Sighing, she makes the sign of the cross and proceeds into the room, where she yanks open the curtains and floods the room with light.

A few more steps forward and she pauses again. She narrows her gaze, slipping the glasses that hang around her neck onto her face. She wasn't wrong to be concerned about the sign on the door. Someone is in the bed.

Carol considers that a joke has been pulled on her. She's seen this before—pillows placed just right, made to look like someone is sleeping under the covers. She calls out. "Sir? Ma'am? House-keeping."

However, as she nears the entryway to the bedroom, she

quickly realizes it isn't a joke. Belongings are scattered everywhere, and furniture is overturned. Silently, she curses the universe for putting her in this situation. This is not the first time she's had to rouse a hungover or jet-lagged guest. Dealing with people is Carol's least favorite part of the job. Two nightmarish shifts at the front desk taught her that much. She vowed she'd never go back.

"Housekeeping," she says once more, this time clearing her throat afterward for added effect. For a second, she debates calling security, or perhaps management, letting them deal with the mess. For the sake of time, and self-sufficiency, she edges toward the balcony, holding her breath. Before she loses her nerve, she peels back the blackout curtains.

As gray light floods in, and the room comes into focus, her hands fly to her open mouth. They manage to stifle the scream. Almost.

There's no mistaking that something very bad has happened in Room 553.

There's the body, of course. But there are other clues, as well. Carol Mesa has seen many strange things while cleaning hotel rooms over the years. But never anything like this.

# CHAPTER ONE

Dr. Max Hastings

BEFORE

"Is it bad?"

"No."

"Did I hurt you?" she asked. Or maybe she said, "Does it hurt?" I can't recall which. Either way, it never occurred to me to lie. I shook my head.

"Are you angry with me?"

"No."

At the time, this was true. There in that hotel room, *everything* was true. My thoughts weren't propelling me too far into the future. I wasn't concerned that her questions might one day become an entity of their own. I wasn't worried that this interaction might come to mean something very different in time. You see, I wasn't bothered with needing to understand. I was, to put it another way, standing where my feet were planted.

"Are you sure?"

I'm fairly sure I hadn't responded. The truth is, I was only half-listening. Warm heat, along with the sting that comes with the breaking of skin, had my attention. Blood beaded at my neck, slowly at first, and then more quickly, finding its way to the surface. I was dabbing at it with a hotel towel, when Laurel reloaded and took aim, firing her next question. Not that I can recall exactly what that question was. I had been thinking about how the hotel staff would wash the blood out. The answer of course, I knew: Baking soda. Mix two parts water and one part baking soda into a paste, apply and let set before scraping off and laundering as usual. Great for organic stains like blood and sweat, as well as materials with a strong smell. White vinegar also worked well: blend vinegar and water and let stained items soak in cold water for up to thirty minutes.

"Max, darling," Laurel purred. "Talk to me."

My brow furrowed as I surveyed my neck in the mirror. The bite was turning out to be less conspicuous than I'd hoped. I checked the time. Sweat ran down the length of my spine. It was hot, and I needed a shower. Since the start of summer, Central Texas had endured record-breaking temperatures. That day had been the hottest day so far— stifling, muggy, and suffocating. The heat could be felt even inside of the hotel; it found us in Room 553, like a fever. It was unbearable. Relentless. It permeated through the walls as though it were a part of them. In turn, it became a part of us.

Of course, it didn't help that Laurel liked to keep the balcony door ajar. She said she appreciated the freedom of being completely there in that room and still having one foot tethered to the outside world.

Eventually, when the bleeding seemed to slow, I turned to her. She was still lying on the ravaged bed, arms propped behind her, her thighs slightly spread. I noticed a thread of semen seeping from the light patch of hair between her legs. Endless legs. She considered me lazily before her gaze moved to the ceiling and then out toward the balcony.

At once, her expression turned pensive. Perhaps she took my silence for anger, but in truth, in so far as I can remember, it was anything but.

To be frank, it had not occurred to me to be mad at Laurel for biting me. That was a part of it, like everything else. And in any case, as I said, I was preoccupied. I was doing what I always did after such encounters: fussing with things, plotting my escape, wondering what was for dinner. I was pondering traffic, and the quickest route out of that room without seeming impolite, ungracious, or worst still, indifferent.

There are a lot of things a woman permits a man to be. Indifferent is not one of them. Anyway, I was too hot, too spent, too completely satisfied to have been indifferent.

Laurel glanced my way and motioned toward the towel I held at my neck. "Do you think your wife will ask?"

I shrugged and turned back to the mirror to reassess the damage.

"Does she ever ask?"

"No."

"Oh...Max." She sighed heavily. "You have the most beautiful shoulders I've ever seen."

My gaze locked on hers in the mirror. I'm certain I smiled.

"What will you say if she does?"

"That I nicked myself while shaving."

Her questions hardly mattered. We were speaking lazily, as one does after making love, bodies spent, minds slightly drunk. This is not to say I would consider what we'd just done making love. With Laurel, what happened between those walls was carnal, primal. Sex without restriction. Nothing more. Nothing less.

I lived a different life in that room. In all of them, actually.

Living was easy. It was no secret that Room 553 was my favorite. I always requested it, saying it was on account of the balcony. Laurel, on occasion, liked to tease me about this. She said a room was a room was a room.

Not to me it wasn't.

Perhaps because it was the first, perhaps because it started with an argument. The kind without words. The kind Laurel and I had a knack for.

It was an afterthought that wasn't. That room had a certain flavor, as did what took place within it. She was different there. Freer, if it was possible—truthfully, Laurel was free just about anywhere.

Meeting in hotel rooms had been her idea. It was nothing personal, she said. This way there would be no memories. No expectations that might have us daydreaming about places or things that might have been. She would never have to remember me in her home, she said, or her in mine, or anywhere where things seemed to really matter. The only space she cared to occupy was my mind, she said. For her, that was enough.

"Do you love me, Max?"

Sometimes, though, she liked to test me.

"Sure."

"You don't know?"

My eyes grazed over her body. Was it love? I don't know. I only know I felt at ease. There was a certain kind of satisfaction in seeing your sweat mixed with that of your lover's, something about not knowing whose was whose, what was what, where you began and she ended. If only for the moment.

Thoughts like those had been going on in my mind.

"Could you see yourself with me?"

I barely registered her words. So, I really can't recall what I said. It didn't help that she was already in the process of luring me back into the bed, both with her eyes and her naked body, her spread legs, her siren's song.

How could I have known that I would relive this scene—conjure this exact moment—hundreds, maybe even thousands of times afterward, and each time from a different angle, from another point of view. For weeks I would struggle to recall the details, and not always of my own free will. More often, others would demand it of me.

# CHAPTER TWO

Laurel Dunaway

Journal Entry

I used to think people who kept journals were pretentious. That was before. I suppose you could say things have evolved. Or rather, I have evolved. Memory is a tricky thing. It's all about perception, and you have to be careful. Perception can be wrong.

It's scary how life has a way of showing you that everything you believed to be true might actually, in essence, be false. The second your life exceeds your wildest dreams, the knife appears at your back.

First, he told me a lie. And then, more lies. A shit-ton of lies. But that wasn't the problem. Lies are normal, when you're a womanizer. The problem was that it was the wrong kind of lie. That's why I have to keep track of them. Hence this journal.

Usually, a person's lies conceal something, and/or protect the person.

Sometimes, a person's lies do both. But not these lies. They didn't do either one. They did the opposite. They exposed him.

He might have thought they'd protect him. They didn't. The lies made things more dangerous. Not just dangerous for him—dangerous for me, too. Which made me wonder if it was an accidental lie. Maybe it was a spur-of-the-moment kind of lie. Maybe it was a lie based on opportunity. A lie of omission. Maybe he lied out of guilt. Or shame. Or insecurity. It's hard to say.

Then, after he lied once, he had to lie again. And the second and third and fourth and the tenth lies were told for the usual reasons. To conceal the first lie. To keep his balls in the air. Maybe that's what it was. Maybe that's why he lied.

Whatever the reason, I couldn't stand by and do nothing. He could have told the truth. Even a tiny truth. He made his bed. He needed to lie in it. Now, it was my turn. It was my move. My chance to advance on the chessboard. But first, I wanted to understand *why*. I wanted to understand the decision behind the lies. You consider the action of a lie and you take a step back.

It's important to look at the decision to lie.

Then take another step back.

What were his choices? What analysis led to that decision? What was going through his mind?

Then, take one more step back.

What information did he analyze to make the decision that led to that action? Then you go back to the action and take a step forward. What result did he expect from lying?

After that you look at intent. Like the courts do. They dole out a variety of punishments depending on reason. When someone gets killed, the court wants to know why. They seek to understand intent. Accidental? Negligent? If so, third-degree. A crime of passion? Second-degree. Maybe third. Malice aforethought? Cold-blooded and premeditated? That'll net you first-degree. The worst kind.

It doesn't even matter if the initial crime was third-degree, if a worse one followed. You're judged on the worst one. If a first-degree crime took place to cover up a third-degree crime, you're judged on the first-degree crime.

*That* he was guilty of. It didn't matter how his lies started out; they had become first-degree. They were told on purpose. Which showed intent. His intent mattered for a practical reason: it was a clue as to how he would proceed.

I needed to know how he would approach things once we were on equal footing.

What would he do next? How would he play his hand? What was his next move?

These were strategic questions on my part, because the answer affected what I would do next. Whether you're trying to make a sale, or win a war, you have to be strategic. You have to ask pointed questions. Loaded questions. Leading questions. This is how you beat them at their own game. You use their answers to predict what they'll do if you do X. If you do Y, you gauge how they might respond. You add it all up and choose the best route forward. You build a strategy. Which is easy, if there's a predictable route for your opponent.

With him, there wasn't. There was a hitch with this particular liar—a hitch that took away the predictable route. A hitch that made it difficult to build a strategy. The hitch was that the liar knew that I knew he had lied. He knew he had been caught. He knew that I knew.

This could only mean one thing: He was already thinking about what I was going to do about it. He was thinking about how bad it could get. He was contemplating worst-case scenarios.

He was thinking strategically. This meant he could deviate from any predictable route I'd considered, and probably would. This made it risky—dangerous.

He's a smart man. Professionally. In all ways that count, really. He'd been in conflict. Conflicts he'd won. Conflicts he'd lost. He understood what all well-trained fighters know: whoever is the first to strike usually wins. If he thought a fight was on the horizon, he'd make the first move. He'd throw the first punch. Which meant I had two choices: wait for him to strike or strike before he did.

He was aware of this, of course. If he anticipated me choosing option two, he'd hit sooner. He would hit before I could. That's the logic of first strikes. If we both thought that going to battle was inevitable, one of us would strike as soon as there was a chance.

A dangerous game.

For both of us.

Which is why I needed a good strategy.

For that, I had to understand his strategy—which was proving to be a real problem. I'd missed it so completely the first time.

# CHAPTER THREE

Dr. Max Hastings

AFTER

"Did she draw blood often?"

Rubbing my sweaty palms against my scrubs, a different kind than I'm used to wearing and yet still kind of the same, I study a sliver of tile that's visible between the table and the chair. When I look up from the floor, I stare unblinkingly at her as she repeats the question. Her voice is monotone, drab and uninspiring, not unlike our surroundings. She utters the words calmly, speaking slowly, as though I simply missed them the first time. As though maybe I really am, as they claim, crazy.

Placing my hands on the table, palms flat, I roll my shoulders and stretch my neck. After, I make sure to sit up a little straighter. She stares at my hands. I follow suit, the both of us wondering what they're capable of. "You wouldn't happen to have any nail clippers, would you?" I ask.

My nails have grown longer than I'd like.

A steely glare is offered but not an answer. We are both aware clippers are not allowed in a place like this.

"Didn't think so," I say before sticking one finger between my teeth, slowly chewing the nail to the quick. Nearly the entire thing comes off. Not as clean as I would like it to, but it will do. I look up at Dr. Jones and smile. "Problem solved."

I don't mean to make her cringe. I don't mean not to, either. It's just, well, our meetings are the least favorite part of my day, and considering my predicament, that is saying a lot.

She doesn't care much for me either. Nor does she bother to hide it. Her face is fixed in a permanent scowl. Although, it is worth taking into consideration that she might be doing that mirroring thing they no doubt ingrained into her during her years of training. Patterns are hard to break, I know, and muscles have memory.

While considering her next question and how I plan to respond, I get the chance to really take her in. She's the kind of woman who could have possibly been attractive once, but has clearly let life harden her through and through. I can't really blame her, seeing where she's ended up.

"Did she draw blood often?" Dr. Jones repeats a third time.

"A couple of times," I say, offering a consolatory breadcrumb. She did show up. I have to give her that. She's reliable—which is more than I can say for the others. If you want to know who your friends are, this is one way to go about it.

"How many?" she asks, and I am careful not to let my eyes wander too far. This is not hard, given the size of the room. Concrete walls, save for the one with the interior window, a flimsy, card-like table, stained with God knows what. Three chairs. Fluorescent lighting. It could have been any room. In any jail. In any city. There is nothing distinguishing about it. Not even the people seated in the chairs.

"Dr. Hastings," she says. Her words hit me in the gut. It's nice, I'll admit, being addressed by my professional name. These days, I go by Inmate 812. "Is the diazepam I prescribed making you feel drowsy? Anxious?"

I shrug. I almost ask what the literature says about how is one supposed to feel when they're caged like an animal. How would she classify the psychology of a person who is fighting for both their freedom and their life simultaneously? What does she expect? Should I stand on the table and dance a jig?

Dr. Jones, with her short brown bob, uninviting scowl, and pencil-thin eyebrows, digs her heels in. "How many times did Mrs. Dunaway draw blood, Dr. Hastings?"

I sigh. While I appreciate the mental stimulation—there's so little of it these days—I hate discussing the intimacies of my life. How could a stranger understand? A psychiatrist, nonetheless.

According to my attorney, I must. I am in deep shit, he likes to remind me. Funny, coming from him. He's not the one spending his days locked in a six by eight foot cell. *Things aren't looking good,* he said, at our last visit. As though it somehow slipped my mind. For what he's charging per hour, you'd think at least a touch of confidence would come as part of the deal. Apparently, it doesn't. *You'd better start remembering,* he'd warned. *Or, on second thought, maybe not. Your lack of recall could work in our favor. Either way, that's what the shrink is for. We need a proper diagnosis. She'll help.*

So far, she isn't helping in any way that I can discern. And I know a thing or two about diagnosis.

"Dr. Hastings." She repeats my name for the third time. "It's imperative that you answer the questions. You're going to have to give me something to go on...and I presume you'd like to see your daughter again?"

I visibly stiffen before I remember I have to relax. This is what they do. Women. They take the things you love, and they use them against you. They're experts. They know how to hit precisely the right pain point. Dr. Jones is proving to be aces at it, which makes me want to tell her everything. Almost. "We only met fourteen times."

"In total? Or in Room 553?"

"In Room 553," I answer, knowing this is a fact she can check.

"Fourteen times in eight months," she remarks, making it clear it's a statement, not a question. I am not surprised by her candidness, the same way I was not surprised to see her when I was called from my cell. I am aware this is her job. I am also aware that she will not give up. She'll keep after me, studying my reactions, coming at me in new and different ways. Maybe she shouldn't care, since she'll get paid regardless. But something about her tells me she isn't that kind of woman. It goes against the core of who she is to cut corners. I know—or rather, I used to know—someone exactly like that. This is what brings me to the conclusion that there is nowhere to go. Nowhere except death row.

I shift in my seat. I can't help myself. Having that kind of weight on your shoulders forces one to do things they shouldn't. Believe me, I know this better than anyone.

"Since it started last November?"

"Correct."

"And how many times did she bite you?"

With a slight shrug, I answer honestly. "Six or seven."

"During intercourse?"

"I think so."

Dr. Jones considers me carefully, fully aware of my hesitation. I had not, would not, perjure myself, and we both know it. It isn't actually a lie. Sometimes it was during intercourse, the biting. Only once after. The day in question, it had been after.

I'd withdrawn from her, rolled over onto my stomach, and inched toward the other side of the bed to check my phone. I had a patient who wasn't doing well, and I sensed I might be summoned at any moment.

Laurel curled at my side like a house cat settling in for a long nap. Eventually, she propped herself on one elbow and peered down at me through half-closed eyelashes. Feeling the weight of them, I turned my back to her. That way I couldn't see her eyes burning holes through me. I could feel them.

Dr. Jones shifts her position. She decides to take a detour, to question me on the days leading up to that afternoon in Room 553.

I had been good, I tell her. This is true. I'd ignored Laurel's texts for two days. Two long and arduous days. What I don't say is that those days were the worst days, up until that point, that I've ever experienced. Minus my current situation. At the time, I hadn't known it was possible to feel anything worse. Turns out, it is.

Back then, I had been a prisoner of another kind. Leaving those texts unanswered took a lot. I could feel the clock, ticking down, like a bomb waiting to explode. Minutes seemed like ages. I could feel the seconds slipping past. Her absence was felt in the marrow of my bones. With each passing minute came the destruction of my willpower. My resolve was wearing thin, even as I tried to hold on.

I made it a point to keep busy. The hours passed, each one eating at me, eroding my conscience, chewing slowly at my core. Thankfully, work was hectic. Work was always hectic. The dying do not stop for the living.

Over the weekend, I made sure my schedule stayed jam-packed. I met Jonathan twice for racquetball, even though he is a far better and far less distracted player than I am, and I hate to lose. Especially to my little brother.

I volunteered to do the grocery shopping, picked up the dry cleaning, and took Ellie to the park. I smiled and swallowed my unease as I watched her on the slide. I pushed her on the swings. I helped her build a dirt castle. A damn fine dirt castle. I had the sense that I was being watched. That I needed to be careful. It just never occurred to me how careful.

Mostly because my mind was somewhere else. All the while, the inevitable was barreling down on me like a freight train.

It had not helped that I'd dreamed of Laurel the night before. A barren dream, endless and desolate, it entered me like an angry spirit, taking hold, refusing to let go until I gave in and fed it what it wanted.

By the time Monday rolled around, no matter what I did, I couldn't exorcise the thought of her skin on my skin, her wry grin, the noises she made when I finally had her where I wanted her. I could think of nothing else. The price for my thoughts: I hated myself on a sliding scale, more and more every single second.

Still, that morning I carried on with it, as you do. I saw my daughter off to school, kissed my wife goodbye, assessed three patients. Patients who were not so much unlike me, dying from something that could not be seen, only felt.

The first half of my day had been, for the most part, uneventful. I held an Ensure to Mrs. Martin's lips and pled on her son's behalf for her to take a few sips. I went through the motions. I wrote scripts for morphine, ordered feeding tubes, monitored dosages, spoke with family members, played God.

As morning gave way to afternoon, as the minutes bled into hours, Laurel was always there, like a nagging memory, in the back of my mind, in the space between breaths. The only bright spot in a sea of monotony. I was careful. Careful to stay focused on work, on dosages, knowing that if I so much as blinked it would be her face I saw in the darkness. Her sighing. Her teeth biting down on her bottom lip, her eyes squeezed shut, her head thrown back in ecstasy. Her coming.

It was a scene that often played on repeat, breaking me down until my mind wandered forward and backward, into the inevitable. The momentum of it carried me until I had no choice but to give myself over to her and her stupid, intrusive, impulsive texts. Until the only thing left to do was to respond—to let what would be, be—to devour her, to swallow her whole, just as she was doing to me.

# CHAPTER FOUR

Laurel Dunaway

Journal Entry

The first thoughts to properly stick were about the timing. Specifically, how very bad it was. The second was the taste of bile rising in my throat. I could feel it. This is it. My life as I knew it was over. He's going to die, and there's nothing I can do to stop it. *This is where it ends*, I thought. This is where I don't get him back. I plead into the darkness. *Not now. Especially not now.*

James would brush it off, if I were to tell him how bad it really got. How far down the rabbit hole I went. If I were to tell him, which I wouldn't—I won't—he would tell me I was overacting. But then, how could he know that? It's hard to say until you get to the end, and we weren't there yet.

In my mind, it wasn't an exaggeration. It was real. It's always real. I pictured a double funeral. I imagined caskets shoved together, placed side by side. Monuments to every man I've ever loved. *God, please don't let this happen now, I said, my fists balled tight.*

The mind works in mysterious ways under extreme duress. In

the haze of being woken from sleep, the pieces of the puzzle rarely fit. It's always the same, and yet, it never is. My heart races. I pray it will all be over quick. Sometimes I trick myself into believing that it might all just be a dream. I have them sometimes —nightmares about losing him.

This time, though, it wasn't that. I can usually tell by the sickly feeling deep down in the pit of my stomach, where if I just heave a bit, the contents of my stomach, even empty as it was, would all come out. This wasn't a fire drill. All of it, all of the thoughts swirling, and I hadn't even opened my eyes.

The alarm chimed persistently, growing louder and louder by the second, reminding me this is reality. This is life and death. Even in the thick of sleep, I was keenly aware it wasn't the normal alarm. It was *the* alarm.

Rubbing my eyes, I checked his Dexcom monitor first. My heart sunk further. Three characters told me everything I needed to know. The situation was dire. There wasn't even a numerical reading. It just read: *low.*

I lurched out of bed, picking up the pace as I half-stumbled down the hall, slowing only when I got to the stairs, then power-walking as I rounded the corner into the kitchen. I opened the fridge, grabbed one of the two-dozen bottles of orange juice we keep on hand, precisely for this kind of situation.

I wiped my sweaty, shaky hands on a dishrag, took a deep breath, and then deftly twisted the cap off the juice. I grabbed a straw from the drawer, flung it in, and made a beeline for the stairs. My bladder clenched and released, making it known my body had needs, too. Although there wasn't time to think about that. I would live. He, on the other hand...

It helped, surely, that my mind had already lurched into the future, ticking off the list of things on my to-do list. *It's Thursday. Laundry day. A medical appointment. Dinner with investors. Or rather, as my husband would remind me, should he live, potential investors.*

*No. Wait. That's wrong. It's not Thursday. As usual, I'm ahead of myself. Today is Wednesday...A dentist appointment. A meeting at Caring Hands. An all-team meeting at the office.*

*Fuck.* It didn't matter, actually. No matter what was on the agenda, I'd be exhausted. Another thought flittered in and then out. *If he makes it.* I could very well be spending the afternoon making funeral arrangements. I shook my head, as though I could push those thoughts away. I'm careful to maintain a vise-like grip on the cold juice as I climbed the stairs, taking two at a time through the dark.

In life, it's important to keep perspective. In a medical emergency, it's not an option. Thoughts about failure like these are inconvenient and pointless when you're neck-deep saving a person's life. The mind, however, begs to differ. It does what it does, drifts where it will. I gritted my teeth, catching myself on the sharp edge of my thoughts. I reeled them in. *My husband needs me.* I know how to do this.

Finally, when I reached our bedroom, I flipped on the light and threw back the covers. His eyelids fluttered.

*What if I can't wake him?*

*Why does he have to push himself so hard?*

I shouldn't feel irritated. After all, I am at least partially at fault, but that doesn't stop me from silently cursing him for putting me in this position. Again. I warned him he needed to slow down. Countless times. I've said it until I am blue in the face. I became *that* wife, the nagging kind. The kind I'd vowed I'd never become. He hasn't been getting enough sleep. He always goes low in the middle of the night when he doesn't get enough rest. Even in an average marriage, there are things you know about a person. Ours is anything but average.

"James," I said, plopping down beside him, attempting to shake him awake. I checked his numbers once again on my watch. Nothing has changed. Not that I'd expected it would.

"James." He didn't budge. "Here," I said, pressing the cold bottle into his arm. "I need you to drink this. You're low."

He shifted, mumbling inaudibly.

"Drink," I ordered, holding the straw to his lips. Thankfully, he obeyed. It doesn't always go so smoothly. The lows are slightly easier that way, but no less dangerous. The highs, I don't want to think about. *I can't think about them.*

I was patient while he emptied the bottle. Afterward, I went around to my side of the bed, fumbled around in the drawer, grabbing what I needed. I didn't even bother with an alcohol swab; I pricked his finger, which started the clock. The countdown began. Ten minutes and I could properly exhale. Fingers crossed.

James didn't blink as I milked his finger, forcing blood to pool to the surface. He had promptly fallen back asleep. Both a testament to his exhaustion and a symptom of the low.

I told myself it was safe to go to the bathroom. *This is all just a waiting game anyhow.* Yet I couldn't force myself to leave him. Not until I see the number I need to see. *Not until it's safe.* Squeezing my thighs together, I distract myself by studying the stubble on his face and the deep lines etched at the corners of his eyes. On the outside, you'd never know how touch and go this can be. My husband is the picture of health. Always has been. Marathon runner, triathlete, successful businessman.

Behind closed doors, life is another story. Being awakened from the dead of sleep in the middle of the night, because if I don't get up he could very well die, is so routine that it's almost normal.

I studied the rise and fall of his chest as he slept. He always looks so peaceful when he sleeps that I can't help but wonder what he dreams of. Certainly, it can't be this.

When the time was up, once again, I checked his Dexcom, the monitor that tells me what I need to know. He only sort of grumbled when I told him that he was still low. He had to drink more juice. I cursed myself for not grabbing two bottles in the first place.

Before hitting the stairs, I considered the Glucagon shot in the drawer. I debated for a second whether or not I should just take a stab at it. It seemed like a no-brainer. Give him the shot. Call 9-1-1. Let my husband's, and thus my own fate, reside in someone else's hands. Someone more capable.

But knowing James would be pissed about taking an ambulance ride uptown, I decide against taking such measures just yet. I head back downstairs for a second bottle of juice.

When that bottle was half-emptied, I waited another painstaking ten minutes before pricking a finger on his opposite hand. All the while, I prayed hard, even though I'm not sure there's anyone worth praying to. I like to hope.

Finally, when my watch chimed and I got the reading I'd been waiting for, I exhaled the breath I'd been holding. Most of it, anyway. I've learned it's important to keep a little something in reserve. Life surprises you less that way.

After I made a beeline for the bathroom, I sat, perched on the edge of the bed for a long while, knowing I wouldn't be able to fall back to sleep. Even though I am bone tired, nerves won't let me. In my mind, the scenario plays like a record stuck on repeat. *What if I hadn't woken? What if it had been too late? What if he had been on a business trip instead of at home in our bed?* So many questions, so few answers. I hear my father's voice. *You can't ask for the storm and get mad when it rains.* Deep sadness washes over me. As I watch my husband sleep, I remind myself I've handled it. He's fine.

*For now.*

I keep my ears perked for the alarm, and I do the only thing I can do to keep myself halfway sane. I write.

# CHAPTER FIVE

Dr. Max Hastings

AFTER

"Tell me about the beginning of the affair," Dr. Jones had asked during her first visit. "I need something to go on." From the beginning, I was impressed by her candor. No need for formal introductions. Pleasantries? Out of the question. Right out of the gate, she went for it. She made it clear that in her mind, I was on borrowed time. "The affair, Dr. Hastings. It's imperative that you tell me everything."

First the police, then a detective, followed by my attorney... even before the angry, bitter psychiatrist, they've all grilled me about it. I haven't spoken to the media, but they have their opinions. I am well aware of that.

The same questions have been repeated for weeks, by other voices, in other places, as summer slowly morphs into autumn.

But something about the way she spoke the words made them feel different than the others.

"The real start?" I had replied to Dr. Jones. "Her father knew mine."

Carefully, slowly, she folded her hands and placed them on the table. She was like the rest of them: impatient, eager for me to get to the point, eager for me to tell her what I wanted her to hear. Like the others, she wasn't trying terribly hard to hide it.

She bowed her head slightly, and her intertwined, extended hands made it appear she was praying. In other words, she was reaching for something she couldn't quite grasp. I couldn't help but smile. Laurel sometimes did that with her hands as I pushed her head into the pillow. I found it interesting how once-welcome thoughts could be tainted by a new kind of unpleasantness here, dissected under the keen eye of the woman in front of me. "No, Max," she said, using my first name, making it personal. "I'm referring to your sexual relations with Mrs. Dunaway. Did they begin before?"

"Before what?"

"Before she married your friend."

"James was not my friend."

From the get-go, Dr. Jones has been impeccable with her jabs. Her disdain for me was made obvious straightaway by a twitch in her right eye. "But you knew him."

"Not really, no."

"Did you sleep together before her marriage? Given that you knew each other?"

"No."

"Not even a flirtation? A kiss? Nothing."

"It never crossed my mind."

"Why not?"

I almost said, because she wasn't my type. This was the truth; Laurel wasn't my usual type of lover. She was a wisp of a woman, tall and lean—nearly supermodel thin, too thin— with pale, milky skin and dirty blonde hair. While her body was firm, especially her breasts, I prefer my women curvy and, preferably, with dark hair. My fraternity brothers back in college sometimes teased me about it. If asked, and I'm sure they will be, they would go so far as to say I have a *type*.

It is a fair assessment. I've always done okay with women. Having, or working toward having an M.D. behind your name, doesn't hurt. Charming co-eds with your medical knowledge and future salary can be quite the aphrodisiac. From college onward, there's a downward trend in happiness for the average female. Women only seem to become all the more disillusioned with life when hit with the reality of life. So, sex, at least for me has never been too hard to come by.

And yet, of all of the women I've known, none have ever given me as much pleasure as she did. I remember the way she laughed, and thinking what a relief it was to hear a woman laugh again. She had a face that proclaimed her sensuality, lightning in her eyes, an avid mouth, a provocative glance. She was both hard and soft, eager and wise. Above all, she was *interested*. She was like a million bucks tax-free. She was an escape, an opportunity. It shouldn't have been this way, but it was. Being with her was not like being with my wife. It gave me a worthwhile feeling, untainted afterward by disgust or regret.

What was there to regret, anyhow? We hardly had time for that. Quite the contrary, actually. After an hour or so of seeking maximum pleasure from each other's bodies, we would dress quickly and get the hell out of there before one of us said or did something we'd regret. We honored it like a ritual.

I remember thinking: *Where had this woman been all of my life? How had I gotten so lucky?* Laurel with her pouty lips, and her tight ass, and her incessant hunger for more. I had never felt more satisfaction than I had then, not only with her, but with everything. Everything counted. Everything had its place in the vibrant universe, including the red welts that often colored her skin afterward. Was it love? Probably not.

But I loved the look in her eyes as she surveyed those welts with a satisfied smile. She always looked as if she had just come from meeting with a lover. She had dark circles under her eyes and she carried with her a great restlessness, an impatient energy emanating from her whole body.

How could I relay this, in a way that made sense to Dr. Jones, without making me look guiltier than I already did?

I haven't yet figured this out. She repeats her question. "Before you were married, before Mrs. Dunaway was married, you've stated there were never any sexual relations between the two of you. Why?"

I couldn't think of another reason, so I offered the closest truth I could find. "I can't say."

"You can't—or won't, Dr. Hastings?"

"I can't."

She shook her head slowly as she jotted something down on paper. I didn't bother trying to read what exactly. When she looked up, she switched gears. "Fine. Then tell me what happened when you ran into her at the care home. Perhaps we should come at this from another place."

# CHAPTER SIX

Laurel Dunaway

Journal Entry

I t started out a shit day. A terrible, relentless, shit day. Probably on account that I was up with James half the night. But *that* was before the real shit part. I'm hardly surprised. November really is the worst month.

Today, he thought I was my mother. He kept saying Debra this and Debra that. The last thing a girl should want to be is her mother. I know. Debra used to tell me that all the time.

Dad spoke of their honeymoon. It was like a horror movie I couldn't turn off. The kind where you very well know what's coming, and you know it won't be good. Yet you can't look away.

I snapped at him. Then I felt terrible. I vowed to do better. Not that it's an option; I know I must. I have to dig deep. Deeper than I've ever dug. I'm just tired.

Tomorrow might be better. But probably it won't.

Today was the first time his disease really got to me. Like properly crawled under my skin and camped out.

*Debra, he said, fetch me my slippers. Debra, sweetheart, where shall we go for dinner? Debra, you look beautiful in that blouse.*

I wasn't even wearing a goddamned blouse. I was wearing one of James's ratty T-shirts and jeans that have grown too loose. I am nothing like my mother. And in any case, how would he know? She was dead long before she reached my age.

For the record, Debra died in November.

I probably shouldn't take it all so personally. His disease isn't a personal assault on my character. That's what James said when I told him.

He didn't know my mother.

Perhaps my husband has a point, though. Yesterday, Dad thought I was someone he knew, back in college. Jamie...or maybe it was Amy. I can't recall. He doesn't either.

To pass the time, I indulged him. I pretended, making sure to nod my head in all the right places. I wasn't half bad at it either. I told him what I thought he wanted to hear. *It's just a game,* I reminded myself, when it very nearly got to be too much.

The kind of game I'm becoming more and more familiar with.

I have to be careful about that, though—about giving away too much too soon. This is why I was careful to save my true feelings for later, as you learn to do. Sometimes I pretend other things too. Sometimes I tell myself it's all fine, and that I'm capable of hiding the parts of myself that need to stay hidden. I'm good at compartmentalizing. I bottle it all, storing my emotions for a time when they can safely come out to play. So far, I have yet to figure out when that might be.

I don't know if it even matters, considering. All I know is that if this is the ending that's coming for me...please—just shoot me now. I don't want to die like my old man.

The thought makes me only slightly more forgiving of Debra for going out with a bang. She died young and beautiful, while she was still on top, which is more than I can say for the rest of us. Especially if I take a look around this place.

Still. I have a lot to live for. So just in case anyone I know happens upon this journal...let it be known... I am not a suicidal person.

I am not my mother.

Obviously, that isn't the answer. I know that.

It's just...yes...sometimes I do think about how easy it would be just to throw up my hands and call it a day. Cop out. Game over. Sometimes I even entertain myself with the manner I'd go about it. I'm coming to find there are endless ways. Humans are far more fragile than we want to believe. I've never told anyone that. But it sure feels good to write it.

Maybe my husband is right...maybe this is too much. Maybe I need to see someone. It's just...well, I don't think that person needs to be a shrink. I'm not crazy. And I don't understand how someone else, a so-called expert even, could possibly have answers about me that I don't have myself.

It seems a bit pointless. Aren't we supposed to grow in wisdom with age? More and more, I am coming to realize, I don't really know anything for sure. How's that for an admission? James would eat it up, for sure.

Maybe this is why I'm writing this down. Maybe it's to prove a point. See? *Look at me.* I'm not losing my mind. I'm still myself. I'm still me. But I'm also someone else.

I guess I sort of have to be.

Every visit, there's less and less of him in the bed.

And in another way, there's less of me sitting in the chair next to his bed.

He's fading away. And there's nothing I can do. My father—probably the only man who has ever really loved me—is just lying there...wasting away, slowly and painfully, for the both of us.

I know that isn't fair to James. He loves me. He does. But not like my dad. Maybe no one can ever really love you like your father. Maybe I'm terrified this is true, and maybe I can't bear the thought of finding out.

And there it is...just another thing I don't know. I should probably start a list or something. Maybe then I'd be less anxious.

I think it's the change. James says it's understandable on account that I haven't been getting any sleep. He says I need to stop taking care of everyone else (himself included) and start focusing on myself. He says I need to get better at dealing with change. He's right, I suppose. I've never cared for change, and I hate this place. *Caring Hands.* It's so cliché it's almost funny. Dad said so himself on one of his good, lucid days.

This is hard for him too. I have to remind myself of that. He doesn't mean to be a burden. He wasn't sick enough to stay in the hospital, and not well enough to be sent home, so here we are.

They're nice enough at least. The place only slightly smells of stale piss. The antiseptic covers it quite nicely. The nurse left a booklet, which I flipped through briefly. It also suggested writing things out. It said it would help. So here I am, doing what I know, keeping records, the same way I do with James's illness, as though a cure can be found in words.

My husband always says you should never put anything in print—that you might as well slit your wrist and bleed onto the page, it's that serious. That's James for you. I've always adored these qualities in him. His petulance—his inability to sugarcoat, to bullshit. It's why I fell in love. It comes in handy at times like these.

He is right. I know. We have to look at the facts. Fact is, my father is going to die. And it's more than likely going to be soon. Hence the reason for moving him to Caring Hands... which...if I'm really being honest...is just a makeshift graveyard.

"Dr. Hastings was here," my father says, causing my pen to halt on the page. When I look up, his expression is relaxed. He seems almost normal, like his old self. This isn't unusual after a nap. I jot that down. Just in case.

"What are you writing?"

"A grocery list."

His expression tells me he doesn't believe me, but he doesn't say it. I ask how long he's been awake. I'm not surprised when he can't tell me. I start to tell him it's okay. I start to say something, anything, when he says, "You remember Dr. Hastings don't you? Max Hastings?"

*Yeah, I remember.*

"He has a beautiful wife and a perfect little daughter," he tells me. "He showed me a picture. Reminded me a bit of your mother and I. And you." It was wonderful, my father says, to see life work out for such a good person.

# CHAPTER SEVEN

Dr. Max Hastings

AFTER

**B**eing in here gives a person a lot of time to think. That's the first thing that really struck me about being incarcerated—how far a day can actually span. How before, when you're on the outside, time seems elusive. Slipping by. Carrying on. Time moves that way. There's never enough of it. Not for all the things you want to do. Not for the things you have to do. I think about this a lot, how I was always rushing, rushing, rushing.

Until one day I wasn't.

Perhaps I should have seen it for what it was. A bad omen. All the signs were there. Really, how could I not have known what was coming?

I can easily recall most of that drive, the vast stretch of sky, the sight of the familiar. Our tree-lined drive, Ellie waiting in the window as I rounded the corner, her little nose pressed to the glass. It reminded me of the day she was born. The day I realized that no matter how great of a physician one might be, there are some things you can't fix.

Nina must have heard me pulling up the drive. Even if she had, she remained in the kitchen. It was Ellie who unlocked the door, flung it open, and stood waiting on the porch. I dropped my things, scooped her in my arms, and asked if she was ready for a swim. When she nodded toward the rocking chair, my gaze followed hers. There on the chair was her stuff, neatly packed, complete with a towel for me, too.

"Did Mommy do that?" I asked, although, of course, I was pretty sure of the answer.

She shook her head, and then all at once her expression changed. That's how my daughter works. Very precisely. So, I wasn't surprised. Not until she pressed her finger into my neck. "Ouch."

Her eyes had grown wide. I'd forgotten about the bite marks.

"It doesn't hurt," I said. "Daddy just cut himself shaving."

I noticed a slight tilt of the head. "And that, my love," I told her, "Is why we don't play with sharp things."

Suddenly, Nina appeared on the porch. "What's this about you cutting yourself?"

I bent at the waist and set Ellie on her feet. "Just a little knick."

Ellie looked up at her mother. Side by side, it was astonishing how much the two of them looked alike. Nina's gaze flittered out toward my car. Her eyes narrowed. "You're not too tired to take her, are you?"

"Nope, I'm just going to grab a water and catch my second wind," I replied shuffling the mess of hair on Ellie's head.

"Good. Because I have to run out. Do you need me to pick up anything?"

I couldn't think of anything I needed in that moment. So I shook my head.

"Okay."

I nodded toward the car. "We're off to swim like the fishes."

"It's with the fishes."

"I'm sorry?"

"The saying," Nina replied. "It's swim *with* the fishes."

"Something occurred at the pool that day? Something that stayed with you," Dr. Jones stated.

"I wouldn't exactly say that."

"But it shook you up?"

I half shrugged. It hadn't really shaken me up. I was trained to deal with that sort of thing. It was my job, in a sense. Ellie, on the other hand—it shifted something in her. That, however, was none of Dr. Jones's business. And I intended to keep it that way.

"Can you tell me what happened that evening? It might help to talk about it."

"A child almost drowned." At night—nights are the longest in here—I sometimes still picture that boy's eyes, fixed and glossy and unmoving. I can still hear his mother's cries. Guttural and desperate. Primal.

"And you saved him?"

"I performed CPR."

Her brow knits together. "The result of which quite possibly saved his life."

"Perhaps." The boy will never be the same, which makes my answer as good as any.

"Wasn't it you who pulled him from the pool?"

"I assisted the lifeguard."

"And your daughter, where was she?"

"I sat her on the edge of the pool, when I saw the boy was in trouble," I answered, even though this has no bearing on anything. Ellie has her issues, but she's a phenomenal swimmer.

"And what happened after?"

"After what?"

"After you saved the boy's life."

"My daughter spoke."

"She spoke?"

"Yes."

Dr. Jones glanced at her yellow pad, at invisible writing. "Ellie is four years old, is that right?"

"Five, next month."

"Speaking was unusual for her?"

"Full sentences, yes."

"And what did she say?"

I looked away. "She said, 'the mommy wasn't watching.'"

"And what happened then?"

"I told her she was right. The mommy wasn't watching."

"YOU WERE ARRESTED NOT LONG AFTER THE INCIDENT WITH THE boy? A few days later? In the pool parking lot?"

"Correct," I say, my eyes closing involuntarily. Even so, memories cannot be erased at will. Not like other things. The image remains. Ellie's little mouth open, formed in the perfect shape of an O. Two female officers forcing her from my arms, carrying her away from me, ushering her toward a waiting SUV. I could see her lips moving, but my ears failed to register the sound. I was fighting, instinctively. I was trying to get to her, but it was pointless. Three officers had me pinned. "Mr. Hastings, you are under arrest for the murder of..."

I was aware of the Miranda warning being read. But my mind was somewhere far off. Meanwhile, my daughter screamed my name.

That's how it happened. How in one day, on a random Tuesday evening, in the dead of summer, life came screeching to a halt. Never to return to the way it was before. And how could it? The events had already been set into motion. Events that had began months—perhaps even years—earlier. They all added up to that one moment.

The minutes and the hours that followed were a blur. My face was plastered all over the news. All over social media. Word spread fast. Given the witch hunt that had taken place, I knew bail would be denied. The notion of being innocent until proven guilty is a platitude that has no bearing once you've been accused.

In the hours I spent in that interrogation room, I came to understand with precise clarity, in a way I hadn't before, that any time a crime is committed—particularly a violent crime against a woman—people want justice. The authorities want to ease the fear of the general public. A quick resolution is demanded from the top down. Politics are involved. Heads will roll. Asses are on the line. This doesn't always lead to the best outcome for those close to the deceased. Fingers are pointed. Accusations are made. Proof becomes easy to come by.

Suffice it to say, there's no going back. Even if I'm found innocent—which I probably won't be—there's no way to undo what's been done. This wasn't simply a case of being at the wrong place at the wrong time. I was *in it*. Deeply involved. They say love is blind, but desire has blind spots too.

Life as I knew it is over. No matter the outcome of the trial, there will always be a cloud of suspicion hanging over my head. Things can never be truly erased from your record. Or for that matter, from a person's mind.

I took that for granted before. Innocence. Anonymity. Freedom.

You don't know what you don't know. Innocence, once lost, can never be regained, and accusations always leave a scar.

I suppose it's hard to appreciate those things. That's what I think about now, most of all. The things taken from me. The ones I can't get back. There's finality that only death can bring.

Although, not all has been lost. At least, not yet. It's important, for one reason—and her name is Eleanor—to hold out hope.

There's still a chance, however small, that the trial could swing in my favor. It's a long shot. But it's all I've got. Which means I have to think like a prosecutor, and a juror—and a killer.

It seems ironic. But that doesn't make it any less true.

~

I USED TO BELIEVE THAT A MAN WITH EXPERIENCE WAS NOT AT THE mercy of a man with an opinion. Now, I know how wrong that kind of thinking can be.

It's half of the reason I don't sleep much these days. It's a scary thing—not so conducive to rest—to put your fate in the hands of twelve of your peers. Peers, of course, being a loose term. I doubt many that serve on any given jury have an IQ that ranges in my vicinity. To serve on a jury, you have to have what? Time.

What do most intelligent people do with their time? Just an educated guess, but probably not volunteer for less than minimum wage. No. They find a way to get out of it. I speak from experience.

You see, thinking, in its simplest form, looks like this: Data-Analysis-Decision-Action.

Notice the end: action. If thinking doesn't end with action, it's useless. Taking action is why we think. Thinking just to think is pointless. That's called daydreaming. Back up one step: decision. We're thinking so that we can decide on a range of options. Simple. Take another step back: analysis. We're sifting through the information needed to make a decision. We're judging the credibility of the information, its reliability. Its usefulness for the decision. And we're combining the new data with what we already know, based on past experiences and our worldview.

Then we're at the beginning: data. We're collecting data. We're gathering what we think will be useful down the line. The information we need to analyze. To decide. To take action. That's the chain of thinking: D-A-D-A. Gathering data leads to analysis.

Analysis leads to a decision. A decision leads to an action. Simple. That's how thinking works.

That's precisely how whether I live or die will be determined. The jury could give me life, and that's what they'll take—all of it that counts, anyway. Or they could sentence me to death. It won't come quick, so I'm not sure the second option is any different than the first.

The third and least likely option is that I could walk.

If I want to see my daughter again, properly that is— untethered, unrestrained, unwatched—I have to aim for a not-guilty verdict. Which means I must not only understand the narrative, but I have to manipulate it *better* than the opposing side.

I have to create doubt in their minds. Not just a little—a whole lot.

# CHAPTER EIGHT

## Laurel Dunaway

### Journal Entry

When you're in sales, you see a lot of strategies. You see big strategies. Small strategies. Worldwide strategies. Strategies across space and time. Then you zoom in, to one market. To one organization. Where intentions collide. Where resources matter. Where histories matter.

Then you zoom in on an individual. A person. Someone with dreams. And fears. And anger. And love. Someone building a strategy to satisfy them all. When you're in sales, you witness a lot of strategies, because that's your job. It's your job to pay attention to big strategies. Small strategies. Regional strategies. National strategies. Most of all, individual strategies.

It's your job to see them and to understand them, because that's how you know when threats to your success exist. To identify threats, you're infiltrating an organization, a person. You're figuring out who is making decisions, and who isn't. You're collecting intelligence on what they know. And what they don't know. You're figuring out their plans. Whether they can help you. Whether they can't. Whether they're a threat. Whether they're going to sink your ship and destroy your plans. Hopefully, you figure that out *before* it happens. You're uncovering their strategy. You're furthering your own. That's the job of a good salesperson.

Most strategies fail because they don't follow the First Rule of Strategy: look forward and reason backward.

Simple, but difficult to do, unless you know a shortcut.

∾

THIS AFTERNOON THE GOAL WAS SIMPLE: TO GET DAD TO EAT. THE good news, he seemed better. More alert, not so yellow. Maybe a little less frail. Perhaps that is wishful thinking, the most dangerous kind, which explains why I'm drawn to it. I've always appreciated a good challenge.

First, we watched an old episode of *M\*A\*S\*H*, which is what got me thinking about my strategy in general, then about how Dad was going to lose the fight, and about how soon that might happen. About how we all eventually lose the war.

Toward the end of the show, he looked over and asked if he'd ever been in the army. There was such a look of sadness on his face as he posed the question that it stirred something inside me, something buried deep, something that thinks it might want to come out. I told him no, he hadn't served. He'd gone to grad school, married my mother. Had me.

He hadn't seemed to believe me, but that didn't stop him from dozing off nearly mid-sentence.

It was a bit of a relief. My plan was working. One can only sit so long watching reruns before one's mind begins to unravel. I was grateful to excuse myself. After checking James's schedule—the calendars on our phones are still synced up, one of the few things that hasn't changed—I text to see if he wanted me to bring him lunch. I knew he'd probably skip lunch if he could get away with it.

There's a deli around the corner from the nursing home, where my feet and my good intentions led me. I grabbed a sandwich, picking up an extra just in case. While waiting on my order, James texted me back. Four words. So simple. So loaded.

*No, thank you. I'm good. Lunch meeting.*

I replied with a thumb's up emoji. It's easier than mentioning that his meeting wasn't on his calendar. Just another way tech makes things both easy and difficult, sometimes simultaneously.

At any rate, it's safe to say, my husband isn't always as thorough as I am.

I picked at my food as I re-read his text, looking for some sort of hidden meaning I knew I wouldn't find. *Lunch meeting.* The words offer no comfort, only the familiar pang of envy I've become accustomed to, down just slightly from the typical twisted, stabbing sensation.

I managed to scarf down half of my sandwich, before trashing the rest. I saved the extra for Dad, just in case he didn't like what the cafeteria was serving.

On the walk back to Caring Hands, I considered making a short detour, dropping by the office. But I thought better of it. There had been a scene the last time, and I realized I'm not ready to show face just yet. It's probably better that way.

"It's nice of you to visit with me," Dad said. "People are so nice at this hotel. They give you all the chocolate pudding you could dream of. They just keep coming around with it...and then sometimes they send wonderful visitors...like you." He furrowed his brow and peered at me like he was letting me in on a secret. "I'll make sure to tell the manager."

Suddenly, a tidal wave of pain swept over me. Searing, red-hot pain. The kind I am typically so good at avoiding. Not then. Not there.

"This is a skilled nursing facility."

"Yes," he said. "I said that, didn't I?" And then, confusion painted on his face, he asked, "Are you sure?"

"Very sure."

"Huh." He began to slap his forehead, over and over. It took some effort, but eventually, I moved his hand away. He did not fight me; instead, his face registered surprise and then something else, something unnamable.

Once again, as though it never left, blinding rage surfaced, infusing my every thought. It was jarring, the way it builds like a tsunami, destructive and inevitable. If my father were going to die —and he is—I don't see why it couldn't happen quickly. Like ripping off a Band-Aid. Instead of this—this slow, torturous, festering wound of a situation, where something as innocuous as chocolate pudding can act as salt.

I was just about to excuse myself to the ladies' room, so that I could throw a proper fit and maybe light a joint, when the man my father was talking about this morning knocked once and then peeked his head around the door.

*Max Hastings.*

Dad lit up like he'd just seen an old friend. He looked at me as though I was supposed to do the same. Strange, because I hardly know Max. Our fathers are childhood friends. Or rather, they *were* friends. Everything is in past tense these days. I think Dad said he died a few years back. I can't recall, and now, neither can he.

"You remember Max, don't you?" my father asked.

I nodded. Perhaps I'd seen him at a fundraiser here and there over the years. Although I wouldn't go so far as to say we run in the same circles. I suppose to say we've hung out on the fringes wouldn't be a stretch.

"Laurel." He greeted me with a tight smile. He folded his

glasses and put them in the pocket of his white coat. I watched his hands.

"Let's take a look," he said to Dad. My eyes scanned the embroidered lettering on his jacket. *Dr. Hastings.*

He glanced up and half smiled, as though he could feel me watching him. Eventually, his long, thick, dark eyelashes fell south as he studied my father. I imagined what he looked like as a boy, even if I can't remember. He shook his head and said, "I was hoping I might see you."

For a second my brow raised, but then I forced myself to look away. Max Hastings looks like the television version of a doctor. Not a real one.

While he finished checking my father over, I studied the bones peeking through Dad's shirt and tried to decide if they're more pronounced than they were this time last week. When the exam was complete, he turned to me. "I'd like to discuss your father's care, if you have a second."

I stood and followed him out into the hall. He looked me over rather intensely, widening his stance, filling up the hall and my consciousness. Finally, he folded his arms across his chest. "Your father has refused pain relief. He states that he wishes to remain lucid. For you."

*Of course he did.* "Dr. Hastings…" I started to explain. But how can I explain my father? How can I take years of knowing someone and compress them down into a few sentences?

"Please," he said. "Call me Max."

I tried to speak, but my lips stuck to one another, as though they didn't want the words I was about to say to come out either. "Max."

He waited for me to proceed. I could see he wanted me to offer him something I can't. Finally, there was a long and heavy sigh on my part. A concession, a waving of the white flag, even though neither of us was quite sure why it needed to be waved. "My father doesn't know what he wants," I told him. "He's half out of his mind."

I shifted my weight from one foot to the other as he considered his plan of action. His eyes ran circles around me, burning holes in my resolve. After a brief eternity, he lowered his gaze. "We're all half out of our minds."

# CHAPTER NINE

Dr. Max Hastings

AFTER

Dr. Jones leans forward, leveling with me. "After you spoke with Mrs. Dunaway about her father's care, what happened then?"

I have her full and undivided attention today. Her mood is lighter—not explicitly happy, but there's something about her that seems slightly more agreeable.

"I went home," I tell her, which is the truth. I had been dog-tired after rounds. I was almost out the door when a page came through about Mr. Dunaway. The nurse was requesting something to help him sleep. It wasn't my finest hour, to say the least. Two of my patients thought it would be a good day to die, and three others decided to give it a trial run.

Needless to say, it was well after dark by the time I made it home. I distinctly recall feeling relieved that Nina had been kind enough to leave a plate for me in the fridge. I don't know what I'd have done if I had been forced to choke down another turkey sandwich. Likely, I wouldn't have eaten at all.

The plate served a dual purpose as well. It meant there was hope. Perhaps the plate was a peace offering, perhaps it wasn't. You never can tell in a marriage. Either way, that evening I found my wife in the bath, and that was a positive sign, if there ever was one.

"You're home late," she said, without looking up. I was neither early nor late. This was simply her way of expressing her disappointment, or seeking reassurance, or questioning my whereabouts. Or all of the above.

"I know," I offered with a weary sigh. It was tinged with remorse. I made sure of it. "I'm sorry. Rough day."

She stuck a toe under the running faucet. "Did you check on Ellie?"

"I did. She's sound asleep. Covers completely on the floor, of course."

Nina didn't look at me. She made it painfully obvious it was on purpose. "She was a tyrant today. Even the sitter made an excuse to leave early."

"I'm sorry," I repeated, unbuttoning my shirt. "May I join you?"

She met my eye then, as I had suspected she would, her face twisted. "Don't you think you should wash the germs off first?"

"I'd planned to."

Her eyes narrowed, and she sort of shrugged, her usual way of icing me out. "Whatever."

From the adjacent shower, I watched her hands as she went through the details of her day. Nina had beautiful hands. Long fingers, like a pianist. She moved them slowly and methodically, painting the air as she spoke. "Ellie refused breakfast, refused to put on a coat, refused help tying her shoes. You'd think she were a toddler, Max," she said. "I have a job—a demanding job. You know how it's been…"

"I—"

Nina pushed herself up to a fully seated position, her breasts causing me to lose my train of thought. She used this to her advantage. Always. "I don't know how much more I can take. We have to do something."

"Boarding school," I said teasingly. We both understood I didn't mean it.

"She needs discipline."

"I don't disagree."

"I'm not so sure about that. We can't just let her call the shots around here on account of—"

"Daddy?" My daughter's voice was followed by her sleepy face peeking around the bathroom door.

"Go back to bed, Eleanor," Nina said with gritted teeth.

"Daddy."

"Your father is in the shower. He's had a long day."

"Hey, pancake." I stuck my neck out from around the shower door. "Go back to bed, and I'll come 'round in a minute to tuck you in."

"Promise," Ellie said, her brows raised toward the ceiling. My daughter only ever spoke a handful of words, but she was recognizing more and more every day, a positive sign.

"Promise."

Nina huffed and slunk down into the water, all the way to her nose. After a several-second stare down to ensure I was telling the truth, Ellie retreated, closing the door behind her.

"You see?" Nina snapped, grabbing a towel. I watched her, with heavy focus on the curve of her left hip as she hightailed it out of the bathtub. "You give into her. It's no wonder she doesn't respect me in the least."

~

"Mommy says you misbehaved today?" I whispered to my daughter in the dark. I needed her to give me something—

anything—to take back to her mother. I do all right with my work. But I am not a man of unlimited means. I cannot afford to send my daughter to boarding school, or anywhere else. Not even if I wanted that, which I absolutely don't. My wife, on the other hand, had been doing her research. She dropped hints like breadcrumbs. Nina had made it clear: she believed our daughter would be better off somewhere else, and she wanted me to believe it too. I could understand her position, even if I couldn't agree with it. Our daughter was getting in the way of her work, and Nina's first love has always been her career.

"Ellie," I repeated. "How was your day? Did you listen when Mommy said to put on your coat?"

Maybe it was wishful thinking, but I'd later swear that Ellie shook her head.

"Listen, El," I said, "It's very important that you do what your mother tells you. If it's cold outside, you wear a jacket—if you're running late, your mother gets to tie your shoes. And you know— I *know* you know—breakfast is the most important meal of the day."

She smiled in the dark, her profile lit by the rainbow light Jonathan had given her for Christmas. Her eyes remained fixed on the ceiling. I sometimes wondered whether she heard me at all. "Promise me, El—that you'll listen to your mother—and Joanie too. Mommy can't rush home from work because you're not listening."

I wasn't expecting a response so I leaned down and kissed her forehead, and pulled the covers tight around her. I tucked them into the mattress as her physical therapist suggested. My daughter's eyes did not meet mine. Aside from the hint of a smile, she gave little indication that she knew I was there at all. "Goodnight, Eleanor."

I was just about to close the door when I could swear I heard her raspy little voice say, "Promise."

~

I FOUND NINA PROPPED UP IN BED, THE COVERS PULLED UP around her.

"She's talking a bit more," I said to her, sliding the covers back. She held up one of her perfect fingers to stop me from speaking. Her eyes scanned the screen on her phone, quickly. No doubt she was doing more of her in-depth research, and no doubt, given her level of anger, she was about to let me have it with both barrels.

"Nina?" I said climbing into the bed. "This is important. We need to talk."

Eventually, she looked up and over at me. "Things don't just get to be important whenever you want them to be."

I was wrong. That night wasn't going to be one of our usual fights. It was going to be the silent treatment. Hence the dinner plate left in the fridge. It wasn't a peace offering. It was a sign. "I understand that."

"So?"

"So, I was trying to talk to you about *our daughter.*"

Her mouth opened and then closed before opening again. She wanted to fight but even she didn't know if she had it in her. "Since when do you care?"

"Come on," I said, keeping my tone even, the way I do with my elderly patients when I'm trying to coax them to do something they don't want to do. "You know that's not fair."

She pulled the covers tighter around her, her arms folded across her chest. Her favorite defensive posture. "Fine, then. What? *What* is suddenly so important?"

"Ellie—she's speaking more."

"And?"

"And it's a new skill. It could explain some of the behavior."

My wife rolled her eyes. "But it shouldn't excuse it."

"I never said that."

With a heavy sigh, she clicked off the lamp. I settled under the covers, feeling the weight of the day beginning to subside. When minutes had gone by and she hadn't offered a rebuttal, I moved toward her, in the dark. I wrapped my arms around her waist and pulled her close. I was aware of the outcome. But that never stopped me from trying. There were good reasons for the effort, and only one of them was the fact that she occasionally gave in.

"Are you kidding me?" she hissed as my hand trailed north. "After the day I've had? Seriously? Not a chance in hell."

I should have stopped there. But I didn't. There's something that needs to be understood about my wife. You're damned if you do, damned if you don't. I pulled her closer and pressed my face into her neck, inhaling deeply. "Thank you for dinner."

I felt her pulling away, eager to resume her normal position, moving swiftly to the other side of the bed. "If you think blanketed niceties are going to get you laid, you have another thing coming."

"I hadn't thought that," I said. "But I could try harder, if it might help."

"That's your problem, Max," Nina told me, the bitterness of her words filling the room like an inky mist. "You don't know how to quit while you're ahead."

# CHAPTER TEN

Laurel Dunaway

Journal Entry

James and I fought last night. A proper knock-down, drag-out fight. It wasn't about normal everyday stuff. We hardly ever fight about that. This time it was about Leo, his prized cat.

I'd been in a hurry that morning, I'll admit. I was distracted by my plan, and I must have left the back door ajar. After a thorough search of the house, it became clear the cat must have wandered out. I could have sworn that I'd closed the door, but as my husband so bluntly put it, who else could it have been?

It hadn't helped that I'd called him over lunch about Dad. He hates to be disturbed at work. If I'd known the cat was missing, I would have kept my best sales job for a better time. Timing is very important. I know because the conversation was brief, and we agreed to leave it for later that evening. Which we did.

The gist of it is this: I want to bring Dad home to die. And by home, I mean to ours. I know it sounds crazy. My husband told me as much.

Actually, he was more succinct. He said I was out of my fucking mind.

He said he never signed up for this.

He said "over his dead body."

Maybe he's right. Still, bringing my dad here seems like the humane thing to do. And to be frank, the easiest thing for all involved. I can't very well keep an eye on things if I have to spend four to six hours out of my day at the care home. That doesn't even include travel.

In retrospect, the answer was right under my nose the entire time, by way of our spare bedroom. So, I checked with hospice. Dad could get the same care in our home, or very close to it, that they give him at Caring Hands.

It's not like we don't have the space, I explained to James. It would be easier. I wouldn't be spread so thin, between home and Caring Hands—and the office, if I ever get back there.

My husband did not—does not—see it that way. He wasn't the least bit intrigued. He was livid. To put it mildly. He accused me of betraying him, of going behind his back, of making decisions about our life without consulting him. I wasn't trying to do any of that. I assured him of this in every way I could. In the end, I wasn't very convincing.

Clearly.

When I went to let the dog out into the backyard, James shoved me out with him. "This," he said, twisting the lock, "is how you properly close a door."

At first, I just stood there with my mouth hanging open. Eventually, he closed the blinds so he didn't have to look at me. I knocked for a good ten minutes, apologizing, pleading, until my sorrow turned to rage. Nothing happened, so eventually I gave up and sat on one of the lawn chairs by the pool. Freezing, I drew my knees to my chest and wrapped my arms around them. I considered my options.

Why hadn't we hid a spare key just in case, I wondered. But then I realized we aren't those kind of people. We don't prepare for the worst. We hope for the best and let the cards fall where they will.

Which meant I'd just have to wait him out. I know James like the back of my hand. Or at least I think I do. He couldn't leave me out there forever. Problem was…I'd only been wearing shorts and a tank top, hardly what I'd need to stay warm in forty-degree temperatures. Minutes passed. And then surely, an hour. The blinds remained closed, and the door remained shut. The colder I got, the more I considered going to the neighbors. I concocted an easy story, demurely confessing that I'd locked myself out. People get off on being the hero, my neighbors more than anyone. They liked the chance to put us in our place and asking for a favor would be a good way to let them do it.

I could show my husband I wasn't kidding. There were only two problems with this strategy: his car was in the driveway, and I'd been crying. Not only did I not want to cause a scene, it was past nine p.m. It wouldn't be fair to inconvenience anyone, as much as I might like to. I have my standards. Nor did I need the complication of witnesses. I did not want to make my husband any more upset with me than he already was.

I just had to wait him out. I am a pro at that. Thankfully. It helps if I don't have to contend with the elements, but as they say, what doesn't kill you, makes you stronger.

I thought I might be superwoman by the time he finally, after an eternity or so of me intermittently knocking, unlocked the door. He opened it and left it ajar. He didn't apologize, and he made it clear— he felt no remorse. I was due a lesson.

What happened next is a long story, but the gist of it is, I caved. I agreed to see someone. It was more than an olive branch. It was the whole tree. If I'd been asked, even just weeks ago, if I'd abdicate control so easily, I would have said never in a million years.

Who knew? Life can change on a dime.

Sometimes you can see the whole picture and sometimes you can't.

"What were you thinking?" he'd demanded. "How could you be so stupid, Laurel? Do you have any idea what it would do—having that kind of responsibility on our shoulders? You can't even keep track of a cat. And you're considering trying your hand on a human?"

*Yes,* I wanted to say. *That's exactly what I'm considering. I've dealt with your health issues for years.* Unfortunately, he beat me to the punch. "Don't you think we have enough to deal with? What if I needed you? How can you not see that you're distracted enough as it is? And Leo. Thanks to you, Leo is probably dead in some ditch —and if he isn't yet—he will be."

"I'm sorry," I said. He didn't hear it.

He was fuming. Pacing the house. Knocking stuff off the walls. This happens sometimes when his blood sugar gets too high. But this wasn't that. "I really don't know what goes through that head of yours…"

"I—"

"No. You know what? I do know," he told me, throwing a dinner plate against the wall. "I'll tell you *exactly* what you were thinking. You were thinking I shouldn't get to have something that makes me happy if you don't have the same. You're selfish, Laurel. You've always been selfish."

"I wasn't thinking that at all." I didn't understand how a conversation that was meant to be about my father had turned into a conversation about an animal. Sure, he means a lot to my husband. I know that. But he's a cat. Cats are resilient. He'd come back. Surely.

"So what then? Let me guess…you thought it was better to

move ahead with things despite how I'd feel. You thought it was better to seek forgiveness than permission."

"No—that's not it."

"That's exactly it." He picked up another plate.

"Forgive me," I whispered, watching the shards of dishware tumbling down around me. "Come to bed. Please. I'll do anything."

"No one," he said, "does *anything*."

JAMES SENT ME A FEW NAMES FROM THE OFFICE THIS MORNING. I texted back right away and agreed to make an appointment. Once my father slipped off into his afternoon nap, I went for a walk in the park, where I intended to do just that. Fresh air can do you good, the nurse told me. It did not do me good. I couldn't stop thinking about last night. I couldn't stop thinking about broken dishes or holes in the wall that would have to be patched. I couldn't stop thinking about what might happen if the cat didn't come back. It was making me sick. As it was, I'd stayed up through the night, making signs, posting on the internet—emailing shelters—doing anything I could. Finally, I threw on three layers of clothes, grabbed a flashlight and went on a search party of one. Meanwhile my husband slept soundly. I expected as much. Things had gotten bad before. But never that bad. My husband could be mercurial. But he'd never locked me out of the house. He'd never ordered me to therapy.

Then, today, while I was in the park, James texted me an address. He'd taken care of the appointment for me. He'd scheduled it for that very afternoon. *It's this or...I don't know...*

It hit me straightaway, like a strong left hook, coming out of nowhere. The realization that my marriage might most definitely be in trouble—that I might not only lose my father but my husband too.

Only it was in a different way than I'd imagined. I'd long considered the possibility of being a widow on account of James's diabetes. But I'd never considered that he might want to leave me on his own free will. The realization was dizzying, seeing his disenchantment spelled out in words on a screen. *You need help. I don't know who you've become.*

All of a sudden, I needed to walk. If I hadn't been wearing boots with a heel, I might have taken off running. I needed something strong and heavy. I needed a distraction. A pick-me-up. Something to take my mind off things.

This is how I wound up in the coffee shop. God knows how far I might have gone had it not presented itself.

When the barista asked for my order, I wanted to say, *"Whatever you've got, just fuck me up."* So as not to be misunderstood, I ordered a quad espresso instead—which I guzzled while scrolling through emails. There were a few from work, but nothing that inspired me enough to respond.

Initially, James had suggested I take some time off, after my father's diagnosis. He thought I should step away from the company we built—let someone else handle my workload temporarily. I won't be able to get this time with my father back, he reminded me. But what had sounded good at the time was, in reality, impossible. Despite our success, we were, in every way that really counted, still very much a lean startup.

It wasn't in the cards for me to take time off. Not now. Not with so much at stake.

Unfortunately, work hasn't been the same. My heart's not in it. No matter how deep I dig, I can't seem to summon the mojo I need—the energy I used to bring. I can't even seem to find the time to look for those things. On the bright side, I'd get to waste an hour I don't have spilling my life story to a stranger that very afternoon. My husband's logic was frequently paradoxical.

I scrolled through my inbox once more. *Delete, delete, delete.*

Isn't it funny, I thought to myself, how the things you once found so important could suddenly become so insignificant.

"Laurel?"

I knew in an instant the voice behind my name, and it wasn't the barista calling out my order.

It was Max Hastings, and he was standing behind me.

I pretended to be surprised to see him. But I wasn't. Not the least bit. Our previous conversation hadn't ended on a high note. When he told me I should consider scaling back on the length of my visits with Dad, I'd told him in no uncertain terms that he could go fuck himself.

"Laurel." He repeated my name as though it hurt to say it. "Listen...I'm....I'm glad to see you here. I—"

"Hello, Dr. Hastings," I swiveled on my barstool, cutting him off at the knee. I'd planned to make a smartass-border-lining-on-rude comment, but on second glance, something shifted in me. There was something in his stance and also, something different. Max Hastings. *Dr. Max Hastings.* Maybe it was the change in environment, or maybe it was something in his expression. Whatever it was, it was enough for me to bite my tongue.

His eyes glanced over me. I peered into them, and it was like looking in the mirror. They were tired eyes, weary even, and yet as intense as any I've ever seen.

"What's up?" I asked coolly. His posture gave nothing away, no indication of what was to come. He seemed like the kind of man who carries himself like he gets laid a lot, the kind of guy who probably loves women, a guy who knows how to properly fuck. It was a crazy thing to think, in retrospect. Considering that I'm married to a man I love desperately, devotedly, irreparably. Devastatingly. Or at least enough to see a therapist for.

"I'm sorry," he offered rather hesitantly. "Forgive me, if I overstepped my bounds. I was only giving my medical opinion. Which I will be the first to admit isn't always the right one..."

More than likely, I rolled my eyes. Max has that effect on me. I wanted him to know that he may have the upper hand at the care home, but there in that coffee shop, we were on equal footing. "In all of my thirty-six years, I can't say I've ever heard a more robust, half-hearted apology."

"My opinion is my opinion," he quipped. "The same with my apology. I say what I mean." He held his hands, palms facing me, in retreat. "Do with that what you wish."

Maybe it was the caffeine. Maybe it was him. I don't know. My heart flung itself against my rib cage like it wanted to leap out of my chest and take him to the ground. The insignificance of those emails and the bitterness of my current situation broke free, and in an instant my irritation was single-handedly pointed at Max Hastings.

Maybe it was settled then. It's unexplainable, which is what also makes it so alluring. What is rational isn't always what takes precedence. All I know is that I refused to let him have the satisfaction of having the last word. I channeled everything—all of it, the uncertainty, the highs and the lows of the last few months—and I aimed them directly at him. "You want to know what I wish?"

He quickly glanced around the coffee shop and then back at me. He sort of shrugged like maybe he'd seen this a time or two. "I wish we could get out of here."

Much to my dismay, I don't think he was surprised by my admission. In fact, I think he knew exactly what was coming. It was obvious by the ease in which he said, "Where would we go?"

"I don't know—" I said. "Anywhere—a hotel?"

His eyes narrowed. But not in the way one would think. It wasn't a rebuttal. It made me hate him and want to eat him alive simultaneously. I hate how self-assured he is. I hate him for not telling me I was crazy like the rest of them. "The Belmond is around the corner."

"Now?"

"Is there a better time for you?"

I checked the time on my phone. "Text me the room number."

I jotted my number down on a napkin. He glanced at it and nodded in the affirmative. And that was that.

# CHAPTER ELEVEN

Dr. Max Hastings

AFTER

"And how did she seem, the first time you met?"
"Who?"

Dr. Jones almost smiles. She's coming to like this cat and mouse game more than she wants to let on. "Laurel. Who else?"

"Young. She seemed very young."

Her eyes shift. "How so?"

"In an inexperienced kind of way. She was very unsure of herself."

"In other words, she was in over her head."

"That's one way to put it."

Dr. Jones fixes her beady little eyes on me intensely. It's nice to get a reaction out of her. These days, it is one of the few things that gives me even a hint of satisfaction. Otherwise, she just blends in with the bland, gray jailhouse walls, like everything else. "I'm specifically referring to the first time the two of you met at the Belmond, Dr. Hastings. How was she?"

I note the way she says my name, like it's poison on her tongue, the syllables shaken and stirred.

"Oh—" I offer a tight smile.

She does not return the favor. "Whose idea had it been to meet there?"

"Hers."

"Are you sure?"

"Fairly sure."

"And how was she when she arrived?"

"Nervous."

"Nervous?" I study the movement of the pen as Dr. Jones jots notes down on her yellow legal pad. She never shows up with the same one, which makes me wonder what she does with them all. I imagine she has a giant stack piled ceiling-high in her office. She doesn't seem like the type who has it all together. Not the way she wants to let on. It makes me question my attorney's motive. Was she just cheap? Or is it something else? If so, I don't see it. Not yet. The read I get on Dr. Jones is that she's the type who has ten cats and piles of clutter spread among the excess of belongings she refuses to get rid of. She's single. And not newly so. Likely every bit by choice as necessity. "Was she always nervous around you?"

"Not really."

"Your father and hers...they were friends...so you must have run into her often over the years."

"Several times, yes."

"And how was this occasion any different?"

"It wasn't."

She glances up and then focuses back on her legal pad. "Had you made advances toward her before that day in the coffee shop?"

"No."

"Did you speak to each other often? At the care center?"

"In passing, perhaps."

"There was no other contact between the two of you? Before you began treating her father?"

"I don't think so."

"But you just said you spoke in passing on occasion."

"While her father was in my care, yes."

"But only in passing?"

"In passing or more personally, it depended."

"During the course of this investigation, it was revealed that Laurel was not the first woman—you indulged in other amorous adventures?"

"I wouldn't call them adventures."

"What would you call them, Dr. Hastings?"

"Whims."

Dr. Jones doesn't mean to show her cards. Her eyes crinkle at the corners, nevertheless. I don't take it personally. I'd bet good money it's not just me. She hates all men. Dr. Jones isn't the only one who assesses people for a living. "These whims...did they occur often?"

"Whenever it made sense."

She jots down something else, this time more quickly. I crane my neck, trying to steal a glance at the page. Her handwriting looks like chicken scratch, making reading it impossible, even for me. "Once with a nurse at the facility where you cared for Mrs. Dunaway's father, is that correct?" When Dr. Jones finishes her question and her note, she makes sure to look up at me. Her mouth is upturned slightly, letting me know she is enjoying herself. She thinks I am a monster.

If she only knew the half of it. "Once, yes."

"Where did that encounter take place?"

"In a supply closet."

Her nose scrunches upward, very nearly touching her brow. She believes, deep down, that she's heard it all. Perhaps it's my job to remind her she hasn't. "At the care facility?"

"Yes."

"And were you rough with her as well?"

"Only as rough as she wanted me to be."

"But it never happened again? With…" She brushes a piece of string from the leg of her pants. I look on as she attempts to pluck the name from memory. "With Ms. Leon?"

"No."

"And why not?"

"Neither of us took it seriously."

Her face remains impassive, but that twitch in her right eye that a little potassium might help remains. "But you had intercourse."

"Yes."

As if on cue, she rubs at her lower eyelid. I wonder if Dr. Jones knows about energy. About the power of suggestion. The power of persuasion. About how to get a person to do what you want them to do, without ever having to ask. If she does, she's not letting on.

"You never did it again?"

"No," I say, noting the way she repeats the same question in different ways. They all do that. The police, the media, legal counsel, lovers.

"Why not?"

"Probably because right after that there was Laurel."

"Do you think Ms. Leon resented you for this?"

"Why would she?"

This time, Dr. Jones observes me with a keener eye. Her expression does not hide her assessment. At best, she thinks I'm an imbecile, simply naive at worst. I won't lie. Her observations make me feel unsettled, as though I no longer know right from wrong.

That encounter back in November, for example. I could sense that Laurel was nervous. I could see that although she was adamant not to let her feelings show, she was in the process of reconsidering. She wasn't sure she should have come. She wasn't sure why she had.

I, on the other hand, was well aware of what led her there. I, never one to let a good opportunity go to waste, was adamant not to give her a chance for second thoughts.

It helped the cause that I wasn't pleased that she was late. Daylight was fading, and I'd promised Nina I'd be home early. We had plans. I hated to let them down.

"He thought I was Doris Day," Laurel said, removing her coat. I removed the Do Not Disturb tag from the interior side of the door, placed it on the handle, and closed the door behind her. "Doris. Fucking. Day. Can you believe that?"

"I've seen worse."

She surveyed the room. "I'll take your word for it." I could see she wasn't pleased by my choice. If she were trying to hide it, she did a very poor job. "From now on, I'm going to have to do my research," she confessed, nervously. "Usually it's someone he knew. Personally, I mean. This one caught me off guard…"

"Can you sing?"

"Not really."

"Next time try that."

I almost got a laugh out of her. She refrained; she held back—why, I don't know. But her shoulders relaxed. The tension in her jaw subsided. "Easy for you to say."

"Nothing is easy for me to say."

Her mouth twisted like she wanted to offer something in response, but couldn't. "Come here," I said. And she did.

# CHAPTER TWELVE

Laurel Dunaway

Journal Entry

J ames went low again last night. Thankfully, he seemed fine this morning. He was up and out the door, headed for the office before dawn.

If only I could summon the energy to follow suit. If only I didn't have to. If only I could stay here in this bed and bask in the memory of what happened at the Belmond. I've been thinking about that a lot—about the difference between wanting and giving in. Turns out, there's not much. I know because that is exactly what I did. I gave in.

The best part?

I don't even feel bad about it. Not that it would be of any use. It was a one-off. It won't happen again.

But, my God, was it exactly what I needed.

Although, I shouldn't write about that now.

Maybe not ever. It's dangerous. If someone were to find this journal...well, it could ruin everything. That's the thing about secrets. They're nearly impossible to contain. Especially over the long haul.

Even so...knowing the risk... something tells me that I have to get it out—that if I don't, the weight of it will eat me alive.

The truth is, I don't know how I ended up in that hotel room, except that I've never wanted to be anywhere more in my life.

It was almost as if some strange energy propelled me forward into the unknown, instead of my own two feet. Into the abyss. And the crazy part? It wasn't even hard to make it happen. To *let* it happen. That's what's scary about the whole thing.

You never know how far you can go. Until you do.

My phone chimed, bringing me back to the present. A text from James. *Can you check to see if the cat food I left on the porch this morning has been touched?*

Eventually, I made my way downstairs. I checked the porch. The bowl of food he left was untouched. I text back. *Bowl is empty.* For good measure, I added the praying hands emoji. And then a smiley face for good measure.

He replied immediately. *Whew. Good to know. Thanks. Keep an eye out, would you? Maybe drive around the neighborhood?*

*I'm on it,* I wrote back.

God, I hate that cat.

God, I hope it comes back. Which is a real shame, because I resent how much James loves it. I know it's not a personal attack on how he feels toward me. But that cat—well, the cat can do no wrong.

Me, on the other hand...

I didn't drive around like I said I would. I did, however, leave the food out until late in the afternoon. Although, when I checked again, there was still no sign of the cat. I trashed the food, burying the evidence. Maybe it was a mistake. I just can't deal with the consequence of telling the truth right now.

This is the thing about lies: you start with one and it cascades from there. Believe me, I know. I never intended to sleep with

Max Hastings. But after days of going back and forth over my father's medication and his "plan of care," what happened between us felt like the next logical step. It sounds absurd, I know.

Sort of like...let's just get this thing done. Let's wash it *and* each other out of our system and get on with it. This way we could be free to focus on more pressing matters—like helping my dad die peacefully, for one.

Obviously, there is a little more to it than that. My life may be in shambles. A real shit-show. But I haven't lost all common sense.

IT WAS NOTHING LIKE I THOUGHT IT WOULD BE. GIVING IN, I MEAN. Giving over to *it* and to him. Max Hastings made it easy.

The second I was through the door, he came at me. It was written on his face—he wasn't leaving it for me to decide. There was no question in his mind what was going to happen next.

I recall being a little disappointed. There was a part of me that had wanted to take the lead, just to spite him. The part of me that despises Max Hastings. Him with his smug grin, his happy, perfect little family, and his need to have the upper hand. I hate the way he's so sure of himself—the way he thinks he knows everything.

I wanted to show him. He doesn't know me at all.

And so I tried. I *really* tried. Then something interesting happened. Something unexpected. Almost as though he were reading me, as though he knew my innermost thoughts, something in him flipped. Like a switch. Something scary, something he seems to be able to turn on and off. Something animalistic. Something predatory.

Something I've never seen before.

Except maybe in myself.

I was mesmerized. How could I not be? It was fucking creepy, the way he stared at me. Like I was the first meal he'd eaten after a weeklong fast. Like he was going to chew me up and spit me out, only to do it all again.

Pretty much from the second I stepped inside that room, all I could think about was that I needed to get out. Bolt. Tell him I'd changed my mind. Do whatever it took to put myself on the opposite side of that door.

Yet, I didn't.

I *couldn't.*

I can't even begin to explain it, not even for a million bucks. I couldn't say why I didn't turn and run. Even if someone held a gun to my head, I couldn't come up with a reason for staying. Not even for a cure to my father's disease. And yet, something deep inside, something all knowing, tells me I really should have gotten the fuck out of there.

Mind control, that's what it was. Hypnosis maybe. Whatever it was—my feet were cemented to the floor. It was like being in the middle of a really good story. It was like I needed to—*no*, like I *had* to—see what was going to happen next.

And, then, I did see. I saw the expression in his eyes, hungry and desperate, but controlled, as he stripped me out of my clothes. Carefully, and methodically, almost like he wanted to put me on display.

For whom, I don't know. He was different in that room, in a fucked up sort of way. He was gentle, so gentle. Delicate. Like I might break if not handled with care. Like I was something to be afraid of. It was uncomfortable—it was disturbing, really. The slowness, the diligence of it all. It wasn't how I'd imagined it would be. It wasn't what I'm used to.

I imagined waltzing into that room, all filled with heat and passion. I imagined there'd be fumbling, and uncertainty— thanks to the careless desire that led us to the Belmond in the first place.

But no. The moment my bra came off, he slowed things way, way down. I hadn't even known such a thing to be possible. I figured he'd be in and then out. He is a physician, after all. They're known for that.

I suppose that's what I found most odd about it all. I'd expected it to be like the rest of my life. Actually, I wanted to tell him to get on with it. I didn't have much time, and I was pretty sure he didn't either. I started to mention my appointment with the shrink, if nothing else as a bit of a warning—just so he knew what he was messing with.

Then, like any good lover, *like any good story*, he surprised me.

"Don't speak," he said, as he peeled my panties down my thighs. "Please."

He took me by the hand and led me to the bed. I was restless, not like myself at all. I realized then that what I'd really come for was a fight and he was in essence silencing me. Is there anything worse than that?

I felt like screaming: this is not who I am. It wasn't just the practicality of it all, or how he had me pinned in all the ways that count, but on account of the fact that he'd reserved a suite. As though this was something other than what it was. Later, far, *far* later, when I brought it up, he said, "It's all they had."

I don't know whether he was lying. Maybe I don't even care.

Anyway, then, right then, in that moment, there hadn't been time for questions. Not only because he'd demanded silence but because he'd shoved me violently back onto the bed, before deftly and one-handedly spreading my knees apart. When he thought he had me where he wanted me, he stepped back and observed me, as though he were committing to memory what he saw.

I assume he was satisfied, because he undressed while I lay there, speechless. I started to stand, to tell him never mind, that I'd made a mistake in coming. Actually, I did say the latter part.

He shook his head. "You haven't come yet."

He pushed me back on the bed. Next thing I knew he was on top of me, gripping my face, his mouth on mine, kissing me so hard it hurt. So hard I couldn't breathe. For a second I thought I might ought to be scared. I thought...*who even knows you're here?*

But I wasn't scared. I wasn't anything. I wasn't Laurel Dunaway, with the dying father or the husband who is sometimes cruel and who needs her too much. I wasn't the thirty-six-year-old who has little interest in starting a family and a waning desire to build a business.

I was someone else entirely.

I was nobody in particular.

As he slipped his tongue in my mouth and ran his hand up my thigh, I let go. Just like that. I let go of whoever it is I'm supposed to be. In an instant, all of my nerves faded into the background. *Everything* faded into the background.

"Do you want me to stop?" he asked.

I didn't, and I told him as much. My words tasted bitter and foreign, like they were coming from someone else's mouth, someone I didn't yet know.

He didn't stop. He buried his face in my thighs. He stuck his fingers in my mouth to stifle me. I found myself scratching at his neck, pulling his hair. Biting. Clawing. Grasping. He didn't care. He didn't ask me to stop. He didn't hold back either. I tried harder. I bit harder, scratched harder, pulled harder.

"You'll tell me if it's too much?" I asked.

He answered breathlessly. "Nothing is too much."

*You don't know me,* I thought.

"I asked you not to speak."

*So, no safe words, then.*

We didn't need a safe word, because nothing was safe and nothing was off limits. Nothing I did fazed him.

Not even when I grabbed him and pushed him inside me. There was no hesitation, no question. He let me have my moment.

Although, not for long. With the slightest shake of his head, he pulled away. He grabbed me by the wrist and ordered me off the bed, where eventually he cornered me against the wall. "You don't get to be in charge here," he told me as he entered me—slowly, at first, and then not so slowly at all.

Whatever I had left in me, whatever anxiety remained, dissolved like ice on a hot day. My sensations returned. My soul felt lighter. My head was suddenly full of more empty space than I knew what to do with. I should have stopped it there, but how could I? I wasn't thinking about the consequences. I was too preoccupied with his ass in my hands, his teeth razor-sharp against my collarbone.

He drove into me angrily, as though possessed by a fever, as though he were desperately trying to reach another place. Somewhere deep inside. Somewhere just beyond.

Afterward, when we were sweaty and spent, I lit a joint and said to him, "We must never do that again."

He'd been fastening his tie. He didn't respond one way or the other. He didn't offer reassurances; he simply motioned with his head toward my hand. "It's illegal, you know."

I shrugged before taking a long, cool drag. I let my head fall backward. All the way back. I exhaled slowly, watching the smoke dissolve into the air. Finally, I looked over at him. "All the best things are."

He seemed faintly disappointed, which I will admit gave me great satisfaction, at least at first, because he wasted no time after that. He washed up hurriedly, but conscientiously, like he'd seen something he didn't like and there was no taking it back. Like maybe he walked the thin line between love and hate too.

I took three more drags from the joint, snuffed it out, and dressed quickly. I got that familiar feeling in my stomach, the one that told me it was a good idea to get out of there before I said or did something I regretted.

"I can't find my lighter," I said, searching the room with my eyes, slipping into my boots. "It's red. Have you seen it?"

Max shook his head. "I'll look for it. I can give it to you next time."

# CHAPTER THIRTEEN

## Dr. Max Hastings

### AFTER

"And what happened *after* that first time at the Belmond?" Dr. Jones asked me quizzically when I'd finished recounting the story. "How did you leave things?"

"I finished up some charting at the office, and I went home."

"And then?"

"And then my wife and I took my daughter to visit Santa."

"Santa?"

"That's correct." For days, Nina had been insisting we get Ellie's photo with Santa. Her own mother had demanded it. Nina wanted to please her mother, and she also wanted to beat the crowds. I'd argued that it wasn't even Thanksgiving, but my wife had vetoed my opinion by telling our daughter about the occasion.

"Did your wife question where you had been?"

"No."

"Did she ever question your whereabouts?"

"No."

"And why do you think that is?"

"I suppose because she was aware of my profession—of its unpredictability and its long hours."

"Did you plan on seeing Mrs. Dunaway again?"

"I was her father's physician, so I assumed I would."

"Did you plan on continuing the affair?"

"That was up to her."

"And how did your wife seem during the visit to see Santa?"

I thought back to that night. Clearly, Nina was under a lot of stress. I know that more now than I did then. Maybe I should have paid more attention, asked more questions. But what good would it have done? The way she felt was apparent in the crease etched deep between her brows. It was obvious in the slight shake of her hands. I wasn't blind. I'm trained to see these things, the subtle nuances that make up a person's physicality. Nina wasn't happy. Her workload had increased both at home and in the office. She felt in over her head. She didn't have to say these things. I was aware of them anyway. Still, I can't say, looking back on that night...I couldn't swear under oath that she was all together *unhappy* either. "She seemed fine."

"Describe *fine* to me, Dr. Hastings?"

I shrug. "She was her usual self."

This is mostly true. Together, we were our usual selves, each of us falling easily into our respective roles. As you do.

"So there was nothing unusual about that night?"

"Not that I recall," I say, which is pretty much how I remember it. We had dinner at Sullivan's, although it was usually reserved for special occasions and also without Ellie in tow. But I can't say it was an anomaly that Nina chose it. Afterward, we'd grabbed hot chocolate from a food trailer. It was a chilly evening, particularly so for that time of year. We went for a walk in the park, the three of us, each cupping our hot chocolate.

On a bench overlooking the lake, I recanted to Ellie the story of the Christmas her mother told me she was pregnant while both she and my wife pretended to listen.

"Did you have sex with Nina that evening?"

*Most definitely.* "I can't recall. Probably."

"Why do you say that?"

"My wife liked to dole out sex as a reward."

"Were you rewarded often?"

I offer another shrug. "Whenever I did something she deemed respectable."

"And taking your daughter to see Santa was one of those things?"

*Yes.* "I suppose."

Dr. Jones looks puzzled. "You didn't think she knew about the other women?"

"I had no way of knowing."

"On your second or third encounter, you told investigators there was something different about Laurel. Can you tell me what that was?"

"She had a bruise on her shoulder," I reply, easily picturing it in my mind.

"And?"

"I asked her what happened."

"So you noticed it straightaway?"

"It was a large bruise."

"What did she say about it?"

"She said she ran into the corner of a wall in the middle of the night."

"Did you question her?"

"No."

"Why not?"

*There hadn't been much time for talking.* "She didn't seem like she wanted to discuss it."

"What did you think had happened?"

"I believed her explanation."

"But then on a subsequent encounter there were more bruises?"

"Yes."

"And those, where were they located?"

"On her back, mostly."

"Did you question her then?"

"Not with words."

Dr. Jones looks disappointed. Or disbelieving. Maybe a little of both. "Then how?"

"You know, other ways."

She cocks her head, narrows her eyes. She's intrigued and yet trying hard not to show it. Although, I'm not sure why. This is her job. "And her response was what?"

"I can't recall. I think she changed the subject."

"Did you suspect she was being abused?"

"No."

"No?" Dr. Jones fixes her eyes on mine. "You see, Dr. Hastings —as a physician—I have a very hard time believing that."

"Either way, it wasn't my place to ask."

"Why not?"

I take a stab at the truth. "I suspected she was into the same things in her home life that we were into outside of it."

"But you still continued to partake in deviant sex, considering?"

"Deviant sex?"

Dr. Jones pulled out her phone. She punched at the screen several times before eventually reading the definition aloud.

*"One. A condition, such as exhibitionism or masochism, in which sexual gratification is derived from activities or fantasies that are generally regarded as atypical or deviant. Two. Such a condition when it*

*causes distress or impaired functioning in the individual or actual or potential harm to others."*

When she finishes, she glances up at me and waits. "Well?"

"Look—" I said, admittedly a little defensive. *That's no definition. It tells you nothing.* "To me, sex is sex. I didn't ask—and she didn't tell. That was our agreement."

"Did you discuss this…arrangement? Or is this just something else that you made up, Dr. Hastings? Another one of your *fantasies?*"

I detect a bit of a personal vendetta in her words. I assume she hasn't gotten laid in some time. "Agreement," I say, correcting her. "And we never discussed it explicitly, no. We didn't have to."

Dr. Jones sighs, as though she is doing me an enormous favor and making a huge personal sacrifice by being here. "You see, Max. I beg to differ."

There was something in the way she said my name. Maybe it was the exasperation in her voice. Maybe it was something else entirely. Whatever the case, an invisible line was breached. I began to feel the familiar pang in my chest that I felt when I was anxious. I thought of it as a butterfly fluttering its wings. She was accusing me of something far worse than murder. Did I care?

The sad truth was yes, I did. I pressed my heels into the concrete to make the feeling go away, and after it subsided, I admitted to myself that perhaps I had to do this. I needed to go there. Perhaps it wouldn't hurt to give Dr. Jones what she'd come for. The thought filled me with something that felt like dread. I imagined this was what grief felt like. "Maybe if we had—"

# CHAPTER FOURTEEN

Laurel Dunaway

Journal Entry

Something about him makes me nervous. *Me,* nervous. I know. I can hardly believe it myself.

I suppose it makes sense. The nerves...the uneasiness I feel toward him. It's not like our last conversation at Caring Hands had gone that well. Considering that he'd been inside me, I expected at least a *little* friendliness on his part during his evening rounds. But no.

There was none of that.

Not that this was completely Max's fault. I was tired.

And I hate doctors, and I hate that nursing home.

But there isn't time to write about that now.

James is due home any moment, and I have to properly hide this. I have to make sure I have time to reapply my makeup and break out of these sweats. Just as soon as I finish this, I'm going to put on something upbeat. James likes to come home to music playing and dinner simmering.

While I'm making a list, it seems…I also hate cooking.

It's just…I don't want him to worry. He's been doing so well for the past week or so. If he only knew what a toll this was taking on me…well, I can't fathom what it would do to him—to us. I only know it wouldn't be good.

That pamphlet from the care home was right. Sorting out my thoughts on paper is a bit of a relief. The therapist only seconded that opinion. I think it was sort of a blessing having the appointment following what happened at the Belmond. Like kismet or something.

Like it was meant to be.

Not that I talked about what I'd done—of course not.

I wouldn't. I couldn't.

At least not yet.

Soon.

Maybe.

AFTER I FIXED DINNER, I WENT TO TAKE THE TRASH OUT, ONLY TO realize that James had left the trashcan around front. I only made it three steps down the drive before I stopped dead in my tracks. *Leo.*

He was laying there on the drive.

As I squinted into the setting sun, I could see him stretched out, basking.

Eyes toward the sky, I exhaled, offering a silent thank you to the heavens.

Upon closer inspection, it became clear that my exhalation had been preliminary. Blood was coming from his head.

I thought at first that maybe he wasn't dead, only injured. I set the bag of trash on the pavement, resting it against my car. I stroked his head gently with my finger, the way I've seen my husband do countless times. He didn't move. I nudged him, turning him on his side. It was then that I saw. The contents of his stomach were gone, eaten away, leaving the cavity filled with maggots. Fat, white, slippery maggots…twisting, turning… I felt my stomach knot up—I knew I was going to be sick. It was so foul, so horrible—so grotesque.

I can't get it out of my mind.

～

AFTER I'D SCOOPED THE CAT UP WITH THE SHOVEL AND BURIED HIM in the flowerbed out back, I used the garden hose to rinse the driveway.

I was worried I might not have time to put everything in its place, but thankfully James texted to say he had a late meeting.

He came home exhausted. As usual. Pronounced he'd had a long day.

*If he only knew.*

His "exhaustion" didn't stop him from going for a long run. I was so afraid he might see something—some shred of evidence I might have left behind.

I was in the shower when he returned from his run. My second of the evening. Maybe it was nerves. Or maybe it was the guilt. Maybe I thought if I didn't scrub myself clean, he'd know. Whatever the case, there I was, standing in scalding water, as though I could somehow wash away what I'd seen. What I'd done. I wasn't even sure if it was the cat or my other sins I was trying to cleanse myself of. All I know is that even if I could wash Max Hastings from my body, I couldn't seem to wash him from my mind.

James slipped in quietly. He asked if I was okay. I jumped at the sound of his voice.

"I'm fine," I said watching as he soaped his body, long and lean and fit, before turning his attention to mine.

"You really need to eat," he said, rubbing his hand along the side of my ribs. "There is such a thing as too thin, darling."

I turned away. "Nice to see you too."

"Come here." He shifted me around. "Don't be like that."

"Like what?"

"You aren't happy to see me?"

"I'm happy," I told him. I offered a faint smile, knowing I should do better. It was all I could muster. He moves toward me, and I flinch. He doesn't seem to notice. He kisses me without question. "You don't look happy."

"Well, I am."

"Good. Because I've set another appointment."

"With the therapist?"

"No."

My stomach flip-flopped. He was right. I did need to eat. But this wasn't that. "By the way…" he said. "How'd that go?"

"Fine."

"That's it?" His brow knitted. "Just fine?"

"It was okay. Better than I thought."

"See?" He smiled. "Not so bad, right?"

I didn't answer.

"So you liked her, then?"

"I said it was fine."

"Did you discuss me?"

I wasn't sure what the right answer was, so I went with the truth. "No. We mostly talked about my childhood."

He seemed surprised. "Not much to unpack there."

"No," I agreed. "Not really." It came out so easily, it might as well have been the truth.

"When are you seeing her again?"

"Tomorrow."

He turned the water hotter.

"Why?"

He smiled, avoiding my question. Then, in the manner in

which he typically avoids things, he leaned in and kissed my forehead. "No reason."

"No, really," I demanded. "Why do you ask?"

He looked me up and down before cupping my breasts in his hands, changing the subject without trying too hard. "They seem smaller."

I said nothing. He was trying to pick a fight. I was doing my best to avoid one. "You know I only want to take care of you, Laurel. Tell me you know that."

I told him I did. And even I wasn't sure if it was a lie.

# CHAPTER FIFTEEN

## Dr. Max Hastings

### AFTER

"Did Mrs. Dunaway ever discuss her home life with you, Dr. Hastings?"

I thought we'd covered this. "Our relationship wasn't really like that."

"So she was secretive about it then?"

"I wouldn't say that. We just didn't discuss the ins and outs of our personal lives."

"But over the course of eight months or so, you met at least a dozen times…"

"Yes."

"How did you feel about Mrs. Dunaway? Would you say you were falling in love?"

"No," I admit. I've only really ever loved one woman—my daughter. But how could I explain that to Dr. Jones without playing into her hand exactly as she wanted me to do?

I couldn't.

So, I offer her the next best thing. "But I sure did like her a lot."

This lands well with her, because there's truth in it. "Laurel was an incredible lover, the kind you wouldn't want to lose."

It isn't an exaggeration. I could hardly wait to be there, in that hotel room, in the moment, nowhere else. I could hardly wait to feel her nails dragging along my skin, her begging me not to stop, her saying she couldn't take anymore. There is no way around it. An itch like that simply has to be scratched.

Dr. Jones looks flushed. Red colors her cheeks. I assume this is why she goes for the jugular.

"Did she ever mention her husband? Did she ever give you an indication what their marriage might be like?"

"No."

"Never?"

I glance down at the table and then back at her. "Never."

She waits for me to say more, and when I fail to deliver, she continues her line of fire. "At what point did Mrs. Dunaway discuss killing her father?"

*About three fucks in.* "I can't recall."

"But you did discuss it."

"We discussed the fact that his expiration was rather imminent."

"You didn't consider that intimate?"

"Not at all."

"See, Dr. Hastings…this is where I'm confused. You want me to believe that your relationship with Mrs. Dunaway was fairly banal." She shifts in her seat. "You make it seem like the two of you hardly spoke."

I check the clock on the wall. Our time is almost up. Unfortunate, because her visits are the only things that keep my mind from scratching itself raw. "We spoke. Sometimes."

"And yet, you don't consider her asking you to aid and abet in a murder to be discussing the ins and outs of your personal life?"

"It wasn't like that."

She glanced up at the ceiling, as if something were written there. A way out of this conversation, perhaps. Or a way in. I had the feeling that Dr. Jones had chosen this line of work because she liked complications. She appreciated its challenges. "You didn't tell the police about it...you've only vaguely mentioned it to your attorney...you don't consider that intimate?"

"I didn't take her seriously."

"But it was serious, though, wasn't it, Dr. Hastings?"

"Not to my mind, no."

"Well, to my mind," she says, gravely, "It makes you seem like you have something to hide."

# CHAPTER SIXTEEN

Laurel Dunaway

Journal Entry

My hand shook as I applied the mascara. I checked my reflection in the mirror, making the decision to skip the eyeliner altogether. I applied lipstick, only to decide the color was too much. *It's all going to be fine. You have nothing to worry about.*

I took several deep breaths. I balled my fists and then released them, the way the therapist told me to do whenever I'm feeling tense. I rubbed my hands together and shook them out. *You can do this,* I said to the woman in the mirror, a version of myself I hardly recognized. James set an appointment. They always made me feel a bit out of sorts. Antsy. Knotted up. Conflicted. I suppose it's always been this way, even in the beginning. That was a part of the thrill of it. Like getting on a rollercoaster. You know what's coming, but there's still the long, slow climb to the top.

The anxiety has gotten worse in recent months. Tonight, I'd

tried to think of everything—of anything—to get me out of it. I pored over every excuse in the book, and yet, I knew that none of them were going to work. I thought of telling James I was sick. I thought of forcing my finger down my throat and making it so. I wondered what would happen if I "tripped" and fell down the stairs.

A little extreme, sure. I just wasn't sure I had it in me tonight. This kind of thing, you have to want it. And I didn't.

What I also didn't want was a fight.

Ironic, considering what was in store.

"That's a bold choice," James remarked, causing me to jump. When I looked up, he was standing in the doorway, eyeballing my dress.

"Is it?"

"It looks great." He smiled before taking a few steps forward and smacking my behind playfully. "As they say, fortune favors the bold."

I watched from the mirror as he went into the closet and picked out a tie. He held it up for me to see. "What do you think?"

"Good choice," I said, because I've learned. The less you say, the more your words will matter.

"Oh, by the way…I noticed the water bowl on the porch…it's empty."

"Is it?"

"Yeah," he drawled. "Mind refilling it before we go? I've got to make a call to the office." He shook his head, as though trying to spring a thought loose. "Something completely slipped my mind."

"No problem." I checked my reflection once more, wiped my sweaty palms on my dress, and wondered how long I could keep this up.

James keeps feeding his dead cat, and I keep half-emptying the bowl. It doesn't make any sense, this game we're playing. If Leo really were eating the food, surely we'd have seen him by now. It seems my husband has been too preoccupied to consider this.

That isn't like him. He knows better. He's not stupid. He's a businessman. *Stay vigilant. Trust but verify.*

I've heard this happens to people whose family members go missing. For a long time after, they set out a plate at the dinner table, they leave their belongings as they were. Eternal signs of hope. Wishful thinking.

I long for that kind of idealism. It was knocked out of me a long time ago. Which makes me wonder if maybe I am more like my mother then I want to let on.

I RECANTED THE STORY FOR DR. MILLER LAST WEEK. IT WAS THE first time I've ever spoken about it, since it happened. To anyone. My husband included. Let's just say James has a different perception of my childhood than the one I actually had. Anyway, Dr. Miller told me that I might consider putting it in writing. She thought it would help.

Imagine a naive little girl. A little girl that knows better, because she's really not that naive at all. Except she is, because she believes the mommy. Imagine she's wearing a brand new dress. It's a thick dress. She can feel the weight of it still—corduroy, because winter is coming. She has tights to match. They're itchy, and the little girl hates them. But the mommy tells her she has to wear them. After all, the mommy has worked so hard to put together the right outfit. It's special, purchased just for the occasion. On the little girl's dress is a stupid turkey. The turkey's feathers are flowers. The little girl loves the dress because her mommy bought it and the mommy says she looks pretty.

Imagine the little girl, with her uneven blonde hair, smiling in her school photo. Picture her baby teeth missing, which she also hates because without them she can't bite her fingernails. Instead, she's taken to pulling out her hair. It's disappearing nearly as fast as her teeth. Her favorite thing in the world is a dirty, stuffed bunny the mommy bought her at a yard sale. It cost a lot. The mommy said a nickel was too much for a girl who misbehaves. Her favorite food—fucking Pop-Tarts.

Imagine this wide-eyed little girl, all buckled into her booster seat. The mommy says a prayer and whispers that this is the last worst day of her life...that they'll be together in heaven.

Picture the little girl smiling at her mommy because the mommy says they're going to play a game. The little girl is supposed to close her eyes and count to a hundred, which the little girl has become very good at. Her daddy taught her.

The little girl does what the mommy says. If not, she goes to the closet, and the little girl is afraid of the dark. She counts to eleven before she notices the mommy is driving very fast. *"Life in the Fast Lane"* plays on the radio. The little girl knows all the words. The mommy really likes that song. *Life in the fast lane / Surely make you lose your mind.* The mommy hums along. *Eighteen. Nineteen. Twenty.* The mommy rolls the windows down. The little girl feels the wind on her face. *Twenty-two.*

At thirty-six, the little girl feels the car accelerate. She thinks about telling the mommy to slow down, but she likes it when the mommy has fun. Sometimes the mommy isn't fun. Sometimes she cries. Sometimes she breaks the little girl's things. Sometimes she doesn't wake up.

*Forty-four.* The little girl's eyes pop open. She doesn't mean for them to—she doesn't want to make the mommy mad— but the car hits something with a jolt, and she needs to know if the mommy is okay. She calls out for her. But the mommy can't hear. The music is too loud. The little girl's dress is getting wet. Her bunny isn't beside her anymore. Water pours in around her. It's cold and it's dark. So very dark. Like the closet. But this isn't the closet. She's sinking. She forces herself toward the window. Her bunny is there. The little girl doesn't know how to swim. She's about to learn the hard way.

# CHAPTER SEVENTEEN

## Dr. Max Hastings

### AFTER

I lied when I said I didn't love Laurel. To tell the truth, in some cases, is a dangerous thing to do. When you're facing a murder charge, love is a powerful motivating factor. And, quite frankly, a complication I don't need. To admit to Dr. Jones, or to anyone, that I was in love with Laurel, would suggest motive. Strong feelings always indicate motive.

Anyhow, there are different kinds of love. According to the ancient Greeks, there are eight different types. But I digress. The point is that attraction and desire—the ingredients that constitute love—are mysterious phenomena, ones even the most advanced scientists have yet to fully understand. Who among us hasn't been blinded by the blanket of emotions that comes from falling down the precipice of union into love?

Obviously, with Laurel, our situation was complicated. I spend hours in here picking it apart, comb over everything that was said, sifting through everything that wasn't, trying to piece it all together like a puzzle.

Some of the pieces are missing, while others don't fit.

For one, we were both in other relationships, and the way I saw it, neither of us had any intention of leaving. The problem with this, as I see it now, is that nothing stands still. Everything either evolves or dies.

Toward the end—and we're getting there—I wasn't sure which I feared the most. Although in retrospect, it hardly mattered. I wasn't the one who got to decide.

Yesterday, my attorney brought a file folder full of evidence for me to sift through. He hopes that it will cause something new to spring to mind. I haven't yet been able to look at it. It's almost nothing I haven't seen before, given my profession. Cadavers are well utilized in medicine. It's how you learn.

Except, in this case, the evidence isn't easy to look at. It's personal. It's taking a look at all the things you thought you knew and realizing you really know nothing. The sad part is I was trained to do that: analyze symptoms, come up with a solution, devise a plan of action.

The world rewards this kind of specialization. But specialization comes at a cost. The trouble is, you learn more and more about less and less until you know everything about nothing. To think outside the proverbial box, you have to be willing to be wrong. You also have to be willing to be right and have everyone *think* you're wrong.

If you suggest an idea that is too boring, no one is going to care; if you suggest something too crazy, no one is going to follow you there. I've been thinking about this a lot at night, lying in my cell—about what I'm going to have to do to get out of here. The cold, hard fact is there's a lot of evidence stacked against me. I haven't figured out how I can prove my innocence when I have no idea how the evidence came to be in the first place. Am I capable of what I'm accused of? Can a person just snap? Can entire parts of our memory be wiped out? I know with my patients that memory loss is certainly possible. But, as my father used to say, putting wings on a bicycle does not make it airworthy. Shoes that don't fit are not a bargain at any price. A good idea that can't be executed is a bad idea. And I am running out of ideas.

THE FIRST TIME ONE OF THEM GOT ME, I WAS ASLEEP. AT THE TIME, I didn't know there were far more rude awakenings than a simple kneecap to the back. Turns out, there are. After that first time, sleep never was easy to come by, and I always fought. Always. Nothing that is taken by force should ever be taken easily.

"You're marked for trouble." I recognized the voice straightaway as belonging to my cellmate. He was a loud mouth but also not one for small talk. He was the kind who got to the point right away. I appreciated that. "I hear you're some fancy doctor."

I was neither going to confirm nor deny his statement. Not until I had further information. Such as why he was posing the question. "Well?" he said. "Is you or ain't you?"

"Who's asking?"

He jammed his knee in harder, and being that I was on my stomach and he was by no means a petite man, I struggled for breath. "Who wants to know?" he mocked. "Who does it look like?"

"Hard to say when you're face down," I managed to choke out.

"You's a wiseass, I see."

*Fuck.* The last thing I wanted him thinking about was my ass. I didn't have much time to redirect the conversation, because he finished his comment with a blow to the back of my head. I was half in this world, half in another. Not totally unconscious, but close enough.

The real bad stuff didn't start that night. Just a little sleight of hand. In terms of what would come later, that night was a breeze.

But it shook something loose in me. It broke a piece off somewhere deep down inside, and I knew it was the kind of thing that could never be put back together again.

# CHAPTER EIGHTEEN

Laurel Dunaway

Journal Entry

"Ready?" James asked, dangling the car keys in my direction. "Jesus, Laurel—you're white as a ghost."

I ran my hands across my face and shook the thoughts away.

"Everything okay?"

"Fine. Just a little tired."

He raised his brow before offering me that boyish, impish look, the one that spreads across his face whenever he's excited. "Eighteen tonight."

*Eighteen.* Generally, there are twenty of us or so. Sometimes more, sometimes less. No one will ask where the missing members are. It's not that kind of club. The rules are simple. The rest is not so.

My husband slipped his arms around my waist. "You look amazing. I'm going to have to watch my back." Another smile. "Yours too."

It's an unconventional arrangement, the club...but then who

really knows, since no one ever talks about these things? Maybe it's more normal than I think. Whatever the case, it works for us.

Over the years, it's grown from about four couples to as many as thirty. At parties, we've had heterosexual couples, bisexual couples, gay couples. The vast majority of us are hetero. It's not that we try to be exclusive of anyone. The other two groups tend to not like to mix.

Only women are allowed to attend alone. Females are far less likely to want to join, to feel comfortable doing so, so it's up to the rest of us to groom them in. Abuse is an acquired taste for some. Oddly, those are usually the ones who tend to stick.

My husband released me from his grip and swung me around so that I was facing him. "What are you thinking?"

"Nothing. I'm just tired."

"So the usual then?"

"What did you have in mind?"

"I have someone I want you to meet."

"Oh," I said, half-heartedly.

"It's up to you, you know—how far to take things."

"Yes."

He motioned toward the door. "Come on. We can discuss it on the way."

I started in his direction, understanding the point he was trying to make. It's all consensual. I suppose you could call what we're into a real life Fight Club for married people, with a dash of fetish thrown in. The gist is, no one is required to fuck anyone. It's like that. We're into a little leather play, a little bondage, a little domination, *heavy* on the domination, and then we go home together, alone. Once or twice—*okay*, three times *max*, in the early days—James and I fucked at a meet up. But usually we don't.

Sometimes I play the dominant party, other times the submissive.

James is never the latter, only ever the former.

He sort of introduced me to the scene, you could say. It wasn't that I was wholly uneducated; I'd just never much cared for an audience where my intimate life was concerned. Although, I have to admit—it was fascinating at first. With James, that was how it was. Everything was new and shiny. My husband never has revealed himself in small ways. He drops bombs. In the beginning, there was a part of me, a big part, that loved this about him. Nothing was ever dull. Hasn't been since.

Over time, however, the allure of the club has waned for me. I wish I could say the same for my husband. He likes to remind me that's a part of it. That's what the game is all about: testing our limits, together and apart.

He's not all wrong. There is something freeing I find about it all. Or at least there used to be. In a way, I go along with it out of hope, the same way James hopes his cat will come back. For me, I'm hoping that the initial draw—the pull, that initial allure— might return. It's like chasing a high you can never quite catch. It's elusive, but it doesn't stop you from trying. That's why I tag along. That's why I don't say no. Marriage is a series of compromises, and this is one of them. My hands might shake, but so long as we follow the rules, so long as we're safe, sane, and consensual, I don't see the problem. Or at least I didn't, until she came along.

WE MEET IN VARIOUS LOCATIONS, USUALLY AT AN ONLINE RENTAL. Airbnb, HomeAway, FlipKey, etc. It's rare that parties occur in the same one twice. Members take turns securing the location. Like I said, it's more simple than you might think, like one of those multi-level marketing pyramids, minus the sales. Like a cult, without the religion. If you're in, you're a believer. It's about mindset. Belief is non-negotiable. *Muscles are strengthened through resistance. Intense heat and pressure creates diamonds. Complete freedom is paralyzing. You need constraints. You need something to rebel*

*against. Known monsters are less scary than unknown monsters.* And so forth.

No one is allowed to wander off in private—and limits have to be agreed upon before the evening convenes. Sex between members isn't off limits, but it's not encouraged either.

In our club, it's seen as a bit distasteful, a bit disrespectful. There are swingers clubs for that. We have tastes of a different kind.

They view what we do there as an art form. Even so, it's not like you would think. Most people don't dress up in leather—or what my husband likes to call slutwear. It's not like you see in the movies. In some ways, I've seen far worse in the sales industry than I've probably ever seen at a club event.

From the outside, before things get started at least, if you were to wander in, you might assume we were having a dinner party, mingling among friends or colleagues. Not that any of us really associate outside of the club; it's not like that either. To be friends, as James says, would be to ruin the fantasy. Boundaries are important in any endeavor.

Boundaries allow us to be whomever we want. This way, we're free to change it up. Nothing is a lie because, other than our fetishes, everything is a lie.

Sometimes even those.

As with most things in our marriage, James is in charge of letting me know when a meeting has been set. He refers to them as appointments. My husband often speaks in code. He likes to test me.

Parties are sporadic. We don't meet on the second Tuesday or fourth Saturday or anything like that. Meetings, so as to keep anonymity, are scheduled less than twenty-four hours in advance. The address is dished out two hours ahead of time. I don't know that there is any rhyme or reason for this, only that it is likely a part of the show. Part of the fantasy. It keeps people coming back.

It makes them feel like they're a part of something special, something exclusive.

James says that to be comfortable, you have to keep things uncomfortable. And vice versa. It's one of the rules. I suppose it makes sense. It's no secret that one of the basic human needs is for novelty, and for my husband and I, the club has certainly fulfilled that.

For me, parties have always been a bit of a release. For my husband, they're a rebellion against middle age, a war-cry against the mediocrity of suburban life. The club bands us together. It makes us feel alive. It makes us feel something.

James has always said that it's hard to have a bad relationship if you have a good sex life, and up until recently, I would have agreed with that.

WE MET TONIGHT AT A TWO-STORY CONDO THE MILLERS RENTED. Or at least that's the name they go by. Who knows who they really are? And, really, who cares?

Sarah Miller is the dominant in their relationship. She gets off on seeing her husband degraded by other women. I happen to be one of them. It's simple enough. It helps that his face annoys me. Everything about him annoys me. I tell him what I really think, and it's easy, because it's the truth. He's a weak man and not because of what gets him off.

Usually, I throw a few punches, pull some hair, rough him up a bit, and then they leave. It's strange to think that the two of them couldn't live out such a simple fantasy at home. But then, who am I to judge?

I was tired after my performance. James found me in the kitchen, leaning over the sink, my knuckles raw and bloody.

"There you are," he said, taking my fist in his hand. He

observed it carefully. "Good God, Laurel. No wonder they were so quick to bail."

I shrugged.

"You ready?"

My face twists to give the impression that what I'm about to say is harder than it is. "I'm not feeling well," I replied. "I was thinking maybe we could head out early too."

He sighed. "We just got here."

"I know. But I feel a migraine coming on...I think I got overheated."

He shifted his weight from one foot to the other. "I think—" he begins, then pauses to open the cabinets, one by one, until he finds what he was looking for. He filled a glass with tap water. "Here," he huffed, holding it out to me. "This will help."

I stared at the glass before meeting his eye. "James—"

His expression was so intense I had to look away. "Laurel... look...I don't know how to say this..."

*So don't. Don't say it.* I willed him to keep his mouth shut.

"But we need this."

"I know."

My answer forced him to relax. "I'm going to hang out with the Bausches. You drink up," he said, nodding toward my hand, "and get some ice on those, and then we'll talk."

I flipped the faucet lever and ran my knuckles under the sink. Anything to avoid looking at him.

"Jane is a fan of yours, you know. You should come."

My gaze stays fixed on my left hand. "I'm going to ice this. And catch my breath. Maybe next time."

He studied me for a moment. I could feel the weight of his eyes on me before giving my shoulder a slight squeeze. "Suit yourself."

I looked up at him. A half-hearted smile lit up his face. "I'm sure you'll be feeling better when I get back."

He was wrong. My head throbbed. The music was loud, too loud, classical with a little jazz thrown in. The point is to make it look as though we are actually having a dinner party. While ball gags are often employed, the odd signal of pain, or pleasure, depending, does occasionally break through.

When my husband is finished with his part, he found me. His eyes were wide-eyed and excited, typical. "Mark showed me a new way to fasten a knot," he exclaimed proudly. "I can show you when we get home, but first— Randall is looking for his favorite little submissive."

"I'm ready to go," I told him.

"We will," he said. "Just as soon as we get you feeling better."

# CHAPTER NINETEEN

Dr. Max Hastings

AFTER

Dr. Jones sits opposite me, crossed-legged, hands folded, resting on the table. "Can you tell me what a typical day was like for you? Before?"

I think about her question for several beats before offering a response. She looks tired today. It appears as though it's taken a lot for her to get herself here.

"On a weekday or a weekend?"

"You usually met Mrs. Dunaway during the week. That would be a fair assessment, wouldn't it?"

"Typically."

"Did you ever meet on a weekend?"

"Maybe once—twice tops. It was difficult to book the Belmond then."

"But you could have met somewhere else."

"I preferred the Belmond. I think Laurel did as well."

"So you consider yourself a creature of habit then, Dr. Hastings?"

"I have an affinity for efficiency."

She looks at me directly before glancing down at her hands. "What happened to your cheek?"

I touched it, unintentionally pointing out the obvious. "Walked into the end of a metal pipe. Crushed the bone."

"It must be tough for you?"

"What?"

"Well—from what you've told me—you're used to being on the opposite end of things."

"I don't see what this has to do with anything."

"Would you say the Valium is helping with the anxiety?"

"Not as much as I'd like it to."

~

CAPITALISM DOESN'T STOP IN JAIL. INCARCERATION IS AN ECONOMY of its own. Like life on the outside, you learn to barter. You learn to sell. You learn the value of things, real quick. You learn to build alliances. You learn if you can't be the strongest, you have to be the smartest. It's a different kind of smart, but intellect, a good sense of business, and good instincts are the kind of commodities one has to possess. It's not so different from the outside in that way—it's the only way to survive.

I learned the value of Dr. Jones fairly early on. As my psychiatrist, she could prescribe medication. Medication was something I could trade. It didn't take me long after that first attack to come up with a plan.

There's a small space at the top of the mouth in between one's molars, the bone and one's cheek that makes for an excellent hiding place. Jailers are smart about this, of course. They don't just hand you your medication without inspecting your mouth. That's why you've got to shove it way, way up there. You've got to swallow convincingly, which is why sometimes, despite my best efforts, I don't always get it right. It's about sixty-forty. Forty percent of the time I have to haul ass back to my cell, position myself over the small sink, and force two fingers down my throat deftly enough that I can still use my hands as a filter. It's a bit of an art form, if you want the merchandise in good condition. Not that it matters. Desperate people do desperate things. They're just worth more whole, is all.

Saving my pills is the only leverage I have against broken cheekbones and all things unimaginable. Things which I seemed to be surprised by more and more as the days go by. That pipe— the one that was smashed against the side of my face—it's used as other forms of punishment too.

Needless to say, I've gotten really good at delivering those pills.

# CHAPTER TWENTY

Laurel Dunaway

Journal Entry

I don't know what possessed me to do it. I suppose it was natural, all things considered. On the way to see Dad today, exhausted and preoccupied, I made the instinctual mistake of turning left instead of right. It occurred naturally, the way it does when you start out driving to one place, but look up and realize you've ended up somewhere else altogether. I wound up at the office instead of the care home.

It felt strange pulling up in the parking lot. Something very simple, something I used to do on a daily basis, was suddenly foreign, as though it were a lifetime ago when being there made any sense.

James had been surprised to see me. He wasn't the only one, in the end.

If only he'd had the balls to discuss the situation with me; then maybe it would have turned out differently. He knows me. Which means he should have known I'm not keen on surprises. Maybe if

I'd been eased into the idea, maybe things wouldn't have unraveled as they did. I plan to tell him as much tonight. The whole thing has me on edge, thinking about what's to come. It won't be pretty.

He should have consulted me. He should have mentioned he'd filled my role. To find my office occupied felt like a slap in the face. As I stood in the doorway to his office—our offices are only separated by a clear pane of glass—he softly said, "It's just temporary. With so much on the line, with the potential sale, we needed the help."

My jaw was practically on the floor. He didn't leave me any room to respond. He stood and walked over to me, leveling himself so that we were eye to eye. He rubbed my forearms and flashed his best sales grin, putting all of that training we'd learned pushing pharma to good use.

My heart raced. It beat against my rib cage as though it might lurch its way up my throat and leap out of my chest. Thoughts swirled—too fast and too scrambled to come out coherently. Somehow they managed. "I don't understand," I said, even though I was beginning to.

"Laurel, please," he pleaded.

My eyes scanned the office. The staff averted their gaze, but it was obvious we had an audience.

"Tell you what," James said lightly, taking hold of my arm as he attempted to usher me toward the front of the building and no doubt out the door. "Why don't I skip out early, and take you to lunch?"

I shook my head, breaking free from his grip, shoving him backward in the process.

He looked stunned. But maybe not really. Without a second thought, I waltzed straight into his office. I searched it, looking for something, looking for *anything*, before settling on the framed photo of me he kept on his desk. He looked at me in that perplexed, funny way he does sometimes. That cat-ate-the-canary look, I like to call it. In this case, I hadn't yet decided who was the cat and who was the bird. Life tends to show you in time. "Laurel," he whispered, his voice milky smooth. "Let's—"

I have no way of knowing what he was about to say. My decision had already flung us into the future. My arm was stretched out in front of us, suspended in midair as I hurled the photo at the glass wall, shattering it. My husband needed to see he wasn't the only one capable of making a mess. "Oh," I said, surveying the damage. "And I forgot to tell you, your cat is dead."

When all was said and done, she just stood there, behind my desk, in shock and clearly afraid. As she should have been.

THE MOMENT I WAS THROUGH THE DOOR TO HIS ROOM AT CARING Hands, I unleashed the weight of what had occurred onto my father. It was one of his lucid days, or so it seemed, and I was thankful for that. I'd called ahead just to make sure. I'd just been dealt one major blow, and I was afraid I couldn't sustain another.

"This place is awful," he remarked as I plopped down in the chair opposite his bed. By this time, we were both aware of how little money could buy when it came to finding a way out. I glanced around the space. He was right. It was awful—drab and tiny. No bigger than a closet. A large walk-in, sure. But a closet, nonetheless.

"You want to know what's awful?"

"Dementia?"

"Yeah. Well, that too. But I was talking about James."

"James? Why?" His expression turned from bitter to one of confusion. For a second, I wasn't sure if it was him speaking or his disease. He seemed to be incessantly slipping in and out of this world these days.

My response came out in a spurt, in exactly the same way it had been lodged in my mind, hardly making any sense. "He hired someone. She was in my office. I went there. On accident or on purpose, I don't know."

"You know—"

I knew what he was going to say by the tone of his voice, and I wanted no part of it. I cut him off. "It's like he's replacing me. It's like he wanted me out. It's like...he saw his chance, and he took it."

"I can see how you could think that," Dad said.

"But?" Max Hastings walked in as the word slipped off my tongue. I paid little attention to his presence; in fact, I hardly noticed him at all.

Dad didn't either, apparently. If he had, he didn't hold his response on account of having an audience. "But maybe you should give him the benefit of the doubt."

I'd expected him to say that. He liked James. Most people do. Also, Dad was known for playing devil's advocate. Max caught my eye. I shifted in my seat so that I was sitting differently, showing my legs to their best advantage. I was distracted, and so was he. But I didn't think it was me doing it to him. He was reacting to someone who wasn't in the room, while I was reacting to him. "Maybe."

"You don't think he's just doing what he thinks is best for you?"

I shook my head. My husband is an opportunist, not a philanthropist. "I think he's doing what he thinks is best for the company."

"That's the thing, sweetheart. Sometimes they're one and the same."

IN VICTORIAN SOCIETY, IT WAS GENERALLY FORBIDDEN FOR A woman to overtly pursue a man she found interesting. The total value of a woman in this era, the only thing that made her seem desirable, was the degree to which she was pursued. If she were thought to be actively chasing a man, it would likely lower her value in his eyes and in the eyes of her family and society. Even though they were stunted by these strict rules, women weren't stupid. They still found a way to approach a man they desired.

If a woman was out for a stroll and spotted a man she'd like to get to know better, she would drop her handkerchief as she passed by, then continue walking. The valiant hero, taking note of the handkerchief that had fallen to the ground in his path, would pick it up and run after the lady to return the item to her, demonstrating that he was indeed a chivalrous, kind, and considerate gentleman. This also provided him with the chance to open a conversation with her, beginning with, "You dropped this, madam?"

The best part? This would allow the gentleman to believe that fate had conspired with Cupid, dropping the white handkerchief of the perfect woman directly in his path. Of course, the woman would know the truth, that she had orchestrated the entire interaction. She chose him, and she made the first move. But it was subtle, simple, and elegant. It was a first move in disguise. Nothing that happened afterward would have taken place had she not dropped her handkerchief.

Today, we have other methods, thank goodness, because I'm pretty sure I don't own a hankie.

After he left my father's room, I texted Max and asked him to meet me at the Belmond. He agreed. In fact, he texted back: If an orgasm is as the French say, a little death, meet me in Room 553 and I'll write your eulogy. Over and over. Until I get it just right.

Later, at the Belmond, we skipped the small talk, not that there was ever much of that. He was mercurial right from the start.

"Laurel," he said. "Do you trust me?"

I had been in the process of slipping out of my jeans. "Why do you ask?"

"I was thinking you might want to take the lead."

I studied him carefully. "Why would I want to do that?"

"No reason. I just thought you might.

"Maybe next time."

"You didn't answer my question."

"I just did."

"I asked if you trust me."

I felt myself beginning to glow, like I'd been on a dimmer that had just been turned up. He was looking for something beyond surface level, and I was happy to oblige. Almost. "I don't really trust anyone."

"That's a shame," he said, glancing toward the balcony and then back at me.

"I don't see it that way."

"You might in time."

"Do you have a point?" I asked. "Or can we just get to it?"

His response was quick, nonchalant. "Whatever you want…"

By this point, we didn't have to agree that anything that happened within the confines of those walls was fair game. It was assumed. That's not to say I didn't understand there was a shift taking place, a changing of winds, as was suggested in his question.

Still, we didn't talk about anything other than what we were doing and feeling in that moment: what we wanted, what we were willing to give. We didn't need to label it or promise a future. Whether that was because it was so obvious to him that we'd have one or because it was obvious we wouldn't, I didn't actually know. For the moment, I didn't need to know, and that in itself was revelatory. I was simply experiencing, and savoring, and growing. Each time we met, I became more myself.

"Laurel," he said, calling me toward him. Max didn't ask permission to blindfold me. He just did. I realized then how close fear and desire live, and how nice it is when you have a little of both.

After he had the blindfold in position, he took my hand and ordered me onto the bed on all fours. I listened as he removed his belt, my other senses heightened on account that I couldn't see, steeling myself for what was to come. He didn't strike me—not that time, anyway. He simply fastened the belt around my thighs and entered me from behind.

I had been close to climax when he pulled out. Max was always aware of this, so I wasn't sure what he was doing. Nor did I have any point of reference. Even with the blindfold, my head had been firmly pressed into the bed. I was half in his world, halfway to heaven, the way he seemed to like it. "Don't move," he demanded as though I'd had any intention of it. I couldn't help myself. I grasped behind me catching air, as I reached for him, pleading without words.

"Does he tell you you're beautiful?" Max asked, his voice throaty and rough. His question wasn't spoken in the usual matter-of-fact way. It wasn't infused with anger, either—a touch of sadness perhaps, but maybe that is just wishful thinking.

I had to think about the answer, even though I knew it well.

"Yes," I answered, softly. Cautiously.

"Good."

I waited, expecting him to say something profound. But he didn't. He removed the belt, flipped me onto my back, and covered my body with his. He searched my eyes briefly and then he placed his hands around my throat and got back to business. He didn't have to tell me what he was thinking. I felt it.

# CHAPTER TWENTY-ONE

Dr. Max Hastings

AFTER

Today, she comes at me from a different angle. "Do you recall the way in which Mrs. Dunaway brought up her father's murder?"

"Her father wasn't murdered."

"Considering the circumstances, I'm sure the prosecution will bring it up...which means it's for the jury to decide. "

"That's fine. But I'm not going to answer a question that suggests I was involved in any way. I haven't been implicated in that crime."

She jots a series of notes down on her legal pad. "I understand. Her father's *death*. At what point did Laurel first bring it up?"

"He was dying from the first moment I accessed him. In a sense, you and I are no different. We're all racing against waning clocks."

"But his actual death, Dr. Hastings? As it occurred."

"She didn't bring it up, per se. Like I said, as his physician, it was evident his condition was declining. It was my job to offer my medical opinion on how to make the process most comfortable."

She cocks her head. "So you see death as a process?"

"It depends."

"My records show it was in late April, approximately, that the final conversation about his care took place."

"That sounds right."

"And how was Mrs. Dunaway? How did she seem?"

"Distraught, slightly."

"Can you expand upon that?"

"She was less herself."

"How so?"

"I don't know. She seemed to have drawn inward some." This was true, in more ways than one. It's not uncommon for people in Laurel's position. It happens. Grief is a nasty beast. And the sad fact was, it did something to me, seeing her like that. An instinct kicked in that I hadn't known I possessed.

Over the span of a few weeks, Laurel's cheeks had sunken in, and her eyes, once vibrant and challenging, were mostly vacant. There was only one place I saw her truly alive, and it wasn't when she was with her father. I don't say any of this to Dr. Jones, of course. It's none of her business.

"After the first time you met at Belmond...you mentioned Mrs. Dunaway said that it wouldn't happen again."

"That's what she said."

"So what led to the subsequent encounters?"

"Usually, she texted me."

"And then what? You'd book a room?"

"Yes."

"How exactly would you classify Mrs. Dunaway's mental state over the course of your sexual relationship?"

"That's not my area of expertise."

She shifts in her chair. "You're aware that you don't have to talk to me, Dr. Hastings?"

"Yes."

"You could just sit silently. Or refuse my visits all together."

"That's correct."

She motions between the two of us. "Then why have you agreed to this?"

"What else have I got to do?"

The truth was, seeing Dr. Jones was better than sitting in a shared cell staring at the same four walls. I hadn't yet been brave enough to leave my cell, even when inmates were allowed out in the common area. Clearly, this would have to change, particularly the longer this situation dragged on. Just not yet.

"Do you understand what's at stake here?"

"Aside from my freedom? My life?"

"You've been accused of murder."

"Keyword being accused. This does not make me guilty."

She threw her hands up. "Well—if that's the case, Dr. Hastings...I suggest you might want to start explaining." She looks down at the table and then up at me. There's a long and heavy sigh, followed by a substantial pause. I think she's waiting on me to say something, but I'm not sure what. Finally, she clears her throat and fixes her gaze on me. "As it stands, there's not much I have to go on. I can only help you as much as you let me..."

"Ah, but you're not really here to help me, are you?"

Her eyes widen. She seems surprised. Or offended. Maybe both. "I'm here to find out the truth."

"You mean whether or not I'm fit to stand trial?"

"That's part of it, yes."

"What's the other part?"

"Your attorney hired me to provide support in your case. It's my job to assess your mental state. He can't do his job if I don't do mine."

"Yeah, well...I don't know what's worse—prison or a mental institution. What do you think?"

"It doesn't matter what I think."

"Ah, you see, it obviously does."

❀

I DIDN'T ANSWER DR. JONES'S QUESTIONS THAT MORNING, BUT I DID spend the rest of the afternoon thinking about them. It was accurate to say I was aware that Laurel was unraveling due to her father's illness. I wish I could say this is a rare thing, but it isn't. Caring for a family member with a terminal illness is no walk in the park. Laurel, though, seemed particularly affected by the ups and downs of it. Not that there are ever really very many upsides to watching someone you love cut out on you. And dementia is about as bad as it gets.

Over the course of that winter, things took their toll on her. She appeared to be growing more despondent and angrier—more attached to me by the day. For the most part, I ignored the changes in her, by pretending not to notice. As a physician, the more you point things out to patients, the more you discuss symptoms, the more those things tend to exacerbate themselves. I thought that by turning the other cheek, it would help.

And for a while, it appeared I was right.

By April, things had shifted for the better. Laurel seemed different, more engaged, more back toward her center, more upbeat, almost hopeful.

She'd brought up the notion of assisted suicide once before, early on, as an afterthought. But it wasn't until April that she first mentioned having a plan.

# CHAPTER TWENTY-TWO

Laurel Dunaway

Journal Entry

The food industry has a term: the bliss point. The bliss point is the optimal level of salty and sweet in a food that keeps you wanting more of that food. They're trying to achieve this all the time. Think kettle corn. Peanut butter. Nutella. What the bliss point achieves is that even though you're getting full, you're never fully satiated. You keep wanting more.

There is a bliss point in relationships. It's possible to make a person addicted in the same way. I know; my entire career is built around this.

The same way there's a bliss point in food and in relationships, there's a bliss point in working someone over.

It's not that I wanted that, per se. I only wanted him. I wanted more.

To get more, I had to have a plan. Attraction follows a formula:

1. Visual chemistry. Animal attraction. It's not just about looks. Charisma, charm, intrigue, mystery, enticement...they all play a part.

2. Perceived value. You have to sell you. You have to ask yourself...how do I show that I have a lot to bring to the table?

3. Perceived challenge. People value what they earn. If it comes too easily, they do not respect it. You must find natural ways to be a challenge. It's not about playing games; it's about creating desire. It's about giving just enough to leave them wanting more.

4. Connection. Initial attraction is one thing—that's easy. That part I had already accomplished. We were fucking. But to maintain desire, you have to level up. You have to get down to what drives a person. You have to ask yourself: what are their core motives? Rather than ask what they do, ask *why* they do it.

James hasn't asked about Leo. I didn't kill his cat. But someone did. I think he thinks that someone is me, and I think he is biding his time. Payback is coming. In the meantime, the traditional method of punishment prevails: silence.

One thing that is becoming clear is that while I am always on guard against people knowing me too much, they wind up knowing me too little. With Max, I understand this has to change. He needs to understand my bliss point. And I desperately need to understand his.

IT WAS THREE THIRTY BY THE TIME I LEFT THE CARE HOME. I KNEW Max would be waiting. I also knew he wouldn't be happy. Even as the nurse tried to calm Dad, I was only halfway present at his bedside. The rest of me was already down the road, thrust into the future, naked in that hotel room. I could imagine Max pacing the room, sitting in the lounge chair adjacent to the bed, reading or doing whatever it was he did on his phone.

He would be annoyed with me for being late, although he

would not say so, and even if I explained the reason, which I wouldn't, it wouldn't change his feelings. Even then, even with Dad in tears, refusing his medication, refusing water, refusing everything—even with him flailing his arms, even with the nurses subduing him, even with the injection of Ativan, I was haunted by thoughts of Max and our last encounter.

I could smell him in the room. I could smell him on my skin. I saw him in places he wasn't. I could feel his fingers pressed into my back, his stubble against my thighs, his eyes heavy on mine.

I'd hoped the nurses might page Dr. Hastings, draw him back here so that we could be in this together. I half-heartedly hoped Dad's outburst might stop the trajectory of what was about to happen down the road. At least then I wouldn't have to leave Dad's room and enter the other one, with its own kind of sickness, just a few blocks down.

Maybe that's bliss. A little pleasure, a little pain. A little uncertainty. Maybe that's how Max has gotten me hooked.

Certainty turns out to be one of the sexiest qualities a person can possess. That's why, as humans, we're so drawn to confidence. Take it away, add a little doubt to the mix, and you create instability. Instability fuels desire. You need a little of both to sustain a love affair.

It keeps the feelings real, which is important.

I've never had feelings that were more real than those that Max provokes. He rides an edge in me, and that edge has dangerous curves. When we met last week, the Belmond had been booked, so we met at the Fairmont instead. He scared me.

In full view of the summer sky, he ran his hands through my hair and pushed my head down between his thighs. "You're late," he said, his dick touching the back of my throat. "My time is valuable, Laurel," he murmured, matter of factly. His actions did not match his tone. "This is something you'll come to understand."

Maybe he thought it was all a game, the way it had been. But I didn't see it that way. It had stopped being fun when I had to repress the urge to vomit and bite down. I should have left. But I was worried. Max calls the shots when it comes to my father's care. I wasn't sure how far he might take things. What might happen if I protested? If I changed the rules?

Later, in the shower, inside me, his palm firmly plastered over my mouth, he used his other hand to pinch my nose. As hot water scalded our bodies, he drove into me, quickly at first and then painfully slowly, so slowly I thought I might die. And the scary thing, I wasn't even sure I'd mind.

~

"Take care of yourself." We weren't speaking; Max was dressing, and I was sulking. "It's important, Laurel."

"Oh?" I offered through gritted teeth. My fists had been clenched so hard I felt my fingernails breaking open the skin on my palms. "Is that what you'd call what just happened? Taking care of me?"

"You shouldn't show up to see your father when you look like shit."

I felt tears brimming, but they had no business in this conversation. *Be careful Max*, I almost said. *Sometimes people bite back.*

"Huh. Well, maybe that's the way I feel."

"Then it will be the way he feels."

"So?" I replied incredulously, his words a gut-check I feel to my soul. "He doesn't even know where he is half the time—and he's dying."

"Yeah, well. He's not dead yet."

I rolled my eyes and began furiously throwing on my clothes. "Is that all?"

"No, actually. It isn't."

I paused in the center of the room in search of my bra.

Max swallowed hard and took a step toward me, cautiously. "I can't stand to see you that way."

I understood the sentiment. He did not seem like the kind of person I wanted to disappoint. And that's how it started. The pull. The sense that nothing else could ever be as potent. That everything else is secondary. Max didn't just tell me, though; he showed me. To a casual observer, it might have seemed illicit, but it was actually beautiful. He was teaching me that sex wasn't about one person being in charge. He was saying that he wanted to move past that. He was telling me I had the power to hurt him too; that love is about sharing power and control, passing it back and forth.

So, that's why I've begun doing my makeup before visiting Dad. I've been making sure to choose my clothing a little more carefully. Each day I hope that Max will notice when he does his rounds, perhaps even pay me a discreet compliment. Only once, earlier this week, I got a cursory glance, and it didn't make me happy. It felt like something punched me from the inside.

# CHAPTER TWENTY-THREE

Dr. Max Hastings

AFTER

"You told your attorney that Laurel had a way of getting things out of you. What did you mean by that?" Dr. Jones inquires.

"Exactly what I said."

"Would you consider yourself a weak man, Dr. Hastings?"

Laurel's name on her lips stirs something in me. Something that quite frankly needs to be disturbed. "Define weak?"

"I want you to think back on your encounters with Mrs. Dunaway. I'd like you to tell me about a time when Laurel won."

This isn't hard to do. Laurel won often. Sometimes I let her.

"I'm hungry," she remarked one afternoon after we'd fucked. Neither of us had been in a particular hurry that day. Although, beforehand she had been angry, full of rage, as she sometimes was.

Sex seemed to allow her to shed that part of herself. "Are you hungry?"

I wasn't feeling anything in particular. "The room service menu is there on the table."

"There's that diner around the corner. I think we should go."

I studied her face. She looked like a beautiful animal, one worth capturing. "Whatever you want."

We'd been to Tony's once, twice tops. Briefly. Each time we'd arrived separately and only to grab a sandwich to go. Food hardly occurred to either of us when we were together. We were after sustenance of another kind. We were both hyper-aware that we were living in stolen moments. We were existing on borrowed time. That afternoon, however, it seemed Laurel was keen on bending the rules. She was asking for more, I realize now, in a way I hadn't then.

"Are you still bleeding?" she'd asked, her eyes on my neck.

"It's stopped."

"What will you tell her, if she asks about it?"

"What?"

"Don't be dense, Max—your wife. What will you say if she doesn't believe the story about the shaving accident? God knows, I wouldn't."

I didn't say anything. How could I explain Nina to Laurel in a way that she would understand? I couldn't. More importantly, I couldn't see why this concerned her so much. Right then, nothing seemed that important. Not even food.

"Did it ever occur to you she was drawing blood on purpose?" Dr. Jones asks, pressing me further.

"Why?"

Later, my attorney would bring it up again. "Do you have proof? Pictures? Anything? It could be advantageous to us to use these injuries in court…"

At the time, I couldn't fathom such things. How could I? When I was completely caught up in experiencing them? That afternoon, I had been answering Laurel in jest, convinced that neither her questions nor the bite marks mattered.

It certainly wasn't anything out of the ordinary. This was just...Laurel. It was what we did. One evening, in late April, after telling me that I had hands like a river, Laurel added that she wanted me to use them on her under the booth at Tony's. She wanted everyone to see what I was capable of.

I smiled, but I wasn't surprised. Laurel always said things like that. She was careless. Or rather she wanted to be.

That spring had produced glorious thunderstorms, and on several occasions she threw open the balcony doors and demanded that I fuck her as the wind blew the rain in. Another time, on a Sunday afternoon, a wedding was taking place down in the hotel garden. We made love to the sound of spoken vows and happy applause.

It was a game, one in which there would be winners and losers.

But not yet.

In that moment, Laurel was naked, standing, stretching, arching her back deliberately and provocatively. Lately it had become her nature to behave in this manner just as soon as the do not disturb sign was hung on the door. She came alive in that room. A switch flipped, something different appeared— like a rabbit from a magician's hat. It's what kept me coming back, and it was at least half the reason why I couldn't stop, even if I'd wanted to.

"Did you feel that you were taking advantage of a woman in a desperate situation?"

*Did I feel guilt? Not really.* Perhaps. Maybe a little. I didn't really give it much thought. "No. It was a mutual exchange."

"You never wondered if she might have had an ulterior motive?"

How can I explain the truth? For one, at the time, I hadn't considered that the hours we were together would be broken down into bite-sized (pun intended) bits of images and words to be peered at under a microscope, not only by others, but by myself as well.

Eventually, I shake my head from side to side. It's not the first lie I've told, and I doubt it will be the last.

# CHAPTER TWENTY-FOUR

Laurel Dunaway

Journal Entry

Dad was not well today. He was worse than not well. He was as bad as I've seen him. The nurse—he has another new one—paged Dr. Hastings, who ordered a bump on his morphine, which put Dad out for most of the afternoon. This was lucky since I couldn't be there on account of my therapy appointment.

Not that I have much experience with shrinks—but I like James's choice well enough. She's unassuming. Pretty, in an unconventional kind of way. Exactly what I assumed my husband would have picked out.

At first, I saw her twice a week. I thought I'd hate it. I thought the abdication of control just might do me in. But it wasn't like that at all. It was a relief. It was nice to have someone to talk to.

Still. To have someone peeking into your life that way, to have them examining your head, dissecting you, exposing you...well, it's just a little over the top sometimes, if you ask me. Not that James has.

I almost didn't show for our appointment today. After last night, the last thing I want is to be exposed. And where do I even begin with that? I can't. There's something about spilling ink that makes it feel real. Maybe I worry I'll find out something about myself I'm not yet ready to know.

Last night we attended a party. Unbeknownst to me, it was our turn to host. James handled it. This meant *she* was there—the woman he hired to replace me at work. The one he's been lying about. Suffice it to say, it did not turn out well. It's ludicrous, given that it was my choice. To be fair, he *had* asked for permission. *That's the thing about you, Laurel,* he said after. *Wherever you go, chaos tends to follow.*

He has a point. Things spiraled out of control. I went too far. I hurt someone. Not intentionally—limits are tricky. Sometimes you can't help yourself. Sometimes accidents happen. Did I mean to break the guy's arm? Did I mean to shatter his nose? No.

But I did.

This has become bigger than me, bigger than I could have ever imagined. Bigger than my husband, even. It's not even like I can pin it all on him, as much as I'd like to. Sure, it might not have been my idea. But I was there. I went along with it. Dare I say—I *even* enjoyed it. Or a part of me did. The part I can never quite access after all is said and done. The part that only seems to be available in the moment. That woman, she rallies. She springs to life. She does what she does. She never considers the consequences.

TODAY, I FINALLY TOLD DR. MILLER ABOUT THE FLING WITH MAX, and even though I explained that I was going to quit seeing him, that it wouldn't happen again, she didn't seem surprised, and I don't think she believed me.

I'm not even sure I believed myself.

"How does it make you feel—the affair?"

"I'd hardly call it an affair. We just fuck. There's no future in it."

"But you feel like this is a betrayal of your marriage," she said calmly. It was a leading question, I recognized. "Why?"

I had to think about it. Really think about it. *Because James would kill me.* She reads my mind. I presume the degree on the wall helps. "Your husband would be angry if he knew?"

"Yes."

"Do you plan to tell him?"

I stuffed my hands between my thighs and stared at the floor while I tried to come up with a good answer. The right answer. Finally, I met her eye. I winced a little to show my uncertainty. "What do you think? Should I tell him?"

"That is the million-dollar question."

"Good thing I came here for answers. That's why my husband insisted on me seeing you, isn't it?"

She appeared confused. "You don't think you need therapy?"

Her words cut like a razor. Even though they shouldn't have. "What I think I need is answers from an objective, professional individual," I replied with a shrug. "Now—how about we just cut to the chase and you give them to me?"

"Ah, now," she said straight-faced. "Where's the fun in that?"

I DROPPED BY THE OFFICE AFTER MY APPOINTMENT. IT WAS A BAD idea, precisely the kind you know you have to follow through on anyhow. I had a sinking feeling that despite patient-doctor privilege, my shrink might spill the beans to my husband. I get it. In her eyes, he's footing the bill, so surely he should get some benefit.

If anyone was surprised to see me, no one showed it. Everything looked the same. Shiny concrete floors, minimalist design, whitewashed walls. It felt good to be there, considering. Almost like stepping back in time. Before sick fathers and strained marriages. Before I began working mostly from home in the pre-dawn hours.

Being there reminded me that nothing is ever as bad as it seems. The glass wall had been replaced, proving all things can be fixed, which I knew. I'd signed off on the invoice.

In the early days, not long after renting the space, James and I painted it ourselves. We worked overnight, cramming it all into one weekend so as not to interrupt things during business hours. We'd ordered takeout and took breaks to make love on the floor, on the desks, on every surface that counted. I can still see the way he looked at me, when he said it would last. I had been nervous about leaving a sure thing for a startup, but James was certain, and he wanted me to be too. It was good luck, he said, what we were doing, christening the place. Marking it as our own. That way, he assured me, nothing could go wrong. Not that we needed luck then. Business had been booming, and even better, we'd finally shed ourselves of our prior entanglements. Things were looking up. It was a sure thing.

Stupidly, I believed him.

JAMES STARTED OUR BUSINESS FROM HIS HOME OFFICE AS A SIDE GIG. At the time, he'd been working in pharmaceutical sales. We were employed by the same company, and although we had different territories, our paths crossed often.

It was at a training conference over drinks that James told me of his idea. He explained with great passion how he wanted to leave repping drugs behind and focus solely on his side hustle. Maybe it was the alcohol, maybe it was his charm, maybe I too was looking for a way out and he seemed as good a ticket as any—

but I believed him. I believed in him. I'd never believed in anything or *anyone* more.

That's how Beacon was born.

Back then, it was different. The idea had been to build a dating site for busy professionals. But like any business, it went through several iterations before we got it just right. It morphed. We morphed with it.

We'd both seen in our line of work how easy it was to find a hook-up. Not so easy to find something—or rather *someone* —serious.

What we came to find, through lots of trial and error, through excessive field-testing, was that busy professionals didn't exactly want anything serious, nor the complications that came with it. It was evident, as with the two of us, that seriousness only led to trouble, to broken hearts, to relationships that needed to be dissolved. People got hurt. It was costly. In all ways.

So, over time, the site morphed until it eventually, and not exactly intentionally, became a site and later an app where professionals could find lovers, serious or otherwise. We broke it down to a granular level, giving members specific criteria they could select from. There are those that are DTF (down to fuck), those that are into FWB (friends with benefits), those that are looking for open relationships, and of course, for the perpetually optimistic, an option for those that are looking for love.

Surprisingly, or not so surprisingly to my husband, the app took off. Beacon went from being a dream to a wildly successful business.

I thought the evolution would stop there. But, of course, it didn't.

ONE OF MY ROLES AT OUR COMPANY IS TO WRITE FOR THE SITE. I write articles and handle communication in the forum, essentially coaching members on how to achieve what they're looking for. Basic psychology. Common sense stuff. Although what's common sense is not always common practice. That's why it's so successful.

I'm working on a piece right now about how to land the lover of your dreams using the psychology of favors.

Benjamin Franklin once famously stated, "He that has once done you a kindness will be more ready to do you another, than he whom you yourself have obliged." This so-called Franklin Effect, put to the test in several recent studies, flies in the face of what most people assume about favors.

It's logical to assume that if someone else carries out a favor for us we feel gratitude toward them and like them better. If someone brings you coffee, or offers to watch your dog, you feel more positive feelings about him or her. But the findings of these studies showed that the opposite was true. When a person carries out a favor for you, it actually makes *that* person like you more. In other words, the person doing the favor for another feels more positive toward them because, in letting them go out of their way for your benefit, you've given them the opportunity to feel better about themselves. Who doesn't want to feel good about them-selves? Who doesn't want to believe they look better in the eyes of the person they're attracted to?

Of course, the Franklin Effect works as long as the favor you ask isn't too out there, or demanding, and you display genuine appreciation. Favors work best if ramped up over time.

The moral of the story is this: people enjoy the validation they receive from being able to please someone else. When this effect occurs between two people with a mutual attraction, the result is intensified, because in asking someone to help you, you've helped to make them feel more bonded to you. It makes the person performing the favor feel chosen—*selected*—and who doesn't want that?

Even if a full-on romantic relationship isn't what members are looking for, the result is the same. Ultimately, they get more of what they're seeking: pleasure.

That's what keeps them coming back.

FINDING A LOVER MAKES FOR A PROFITABLE BUSINESS FOR THE simple fact that most people live far below their potential. Not because they don't have the capacity to achieve more, and not because they have not been given authority over their life. Most people are living like they're living because they don't believe they can have anymore than they have right now. They want to believe; they just can't see past reality. It doesn't help that history is a strong indicator. That's where Beacon comes in.

There's an old saying: If you can determine what a man will think, you never have to concern yourself with what he will do. If you can make a man feel inferior, you never have to compel him to seek an inferior status; he will seek it himself.

Jobs. Relationships. Finances. Take any area of a person's life, look at their beliefs about those things, and it will show you the quality of that area.

The sad fact is most people lack imagination.

I am not one of those people.

IN THE AFTERNOON, I TEXTED MAX. I WANTED TO SEE HIM. I *needed* to see him. As usual, he booked a room at the Belmond. Max is like most people, a creature of habit. He likes things easy. When I brought this up, playfully, of course, he said there were other places, if I wanted. I didn't. To have said otherwise would have been a mistake. You can't tell people what you want. You have to show them.

Anyhow, he didn't expand on what sort of places he had in

mind, and I hadn't asked him to. I like the simplicity of hotels. I'm not a backseat kind of girl. I'm not in it for the danger. I'm in it for the distraction.

He'd thought the sex couldn't get any better, but I've learned how to break him in slowly, like a good pair of shoes.

I fucked him senseless, on and against every surface of that room. He seemed grateful for my thoroughness. I, on the other hand, was grateful it hadn't been like the last time. Slow and torturous. Holy and sanctimonious.

"You don't have to have divine sex everyday," I told him afterward. "Sometimes you just need to fuck."

"Right," he'd said, his expression half-amused, half-perplexed.

"I have to get back to work."

"Me, too."

I slipped my dress over my head. "But first, I need to know how long my dad has left."

He was pulling on his scrubs when he paused and looked over at me. "Hard to say."

"Is there a way to speed things up?"

"Dementia is a progressive disease."

"I know that, Max. What I'm asking is how long can this take?"

"As long as it takes," he answered. He softened it in an almost unnatural way by adding, "Unfortunately."

"Yeah but how long does he have to suffer?"

"It's not an exact science. Things live and die at their own pace."

Somehow I seemed to know that better than anyone.

I walked over to the mirror and piled my hair on top of my head, holding it in place with my hand. "How much morphine would it take to kill a person?"

"Morphine?" Max studied my reflection in the mirror. Eventually, he cocked his head. "I wouldn't use morphine. Though it's possible, there are easier ways."

"Such as?"

"Well, a combination of barbiturates and potassium chloride usually does the trick."

I let my hair fall around my shoulders. "Where would one come by those things?"

"Do you have a veterinarian?" he asked blandly, because, well, that is Max's way.

I walked over to where he was standing, turned my back toward him, and motioned for him to zip my dress. "It just so happens I do."

# CHAPTER TWENTY-FIVE

Dr. Max Hastings

AFTER

B reathless, Laurel said, "Could you see us doing this for the rest of our lives?"

We'd just had the most exhaustive kind of sex and, having just come off a twenty-four hour call, I was spent. I was thinking about going home, crawling into bed, and sleeping the day away. "Sure."

"It doesn't scare you?"

"Why would it?"

She stared at me disbelievingly. "How would we ever get anything done?"

"We get a lot done, if you ask me."

"Can you imagine what it would be like if we were together, *together?*"

That question, so lightly pressed that day, would crop up again and again, and would turn so threatening in time. In that moment, like the rest, it was a just game. Pure fantasy.

"We'd settle in."

She cocked one brow. "Into what?"

"Life," I said heading toward the bathroom.

I showered that afternoon. She hadn't. Afterward, the two of us headed to Tony's. Laurel insisted we share a milkshake in a booth. For the sake of posterity, she'd said. At the time, I didn't see any harm in indulging her. It was a particularly hot day, and I had been hungry. Call had been particularly brutal. Three patients coded, three families to deal with. Lots of charting left to do. And anyhow, after what we'd just experienced, ice cream seemed like the least I could do.

I paid for the shake, double chocolate at Laurel's request, and the two of us settled into a booth.

"Answer me honestly Max. If I were single…"

As I studied her lips puckered around the straw, my thoughts flittered back to the first time I saw her—*really* saw her. I was thinking about how sad she looked and how a woman that beautiful should never look that sad. I recall being well aware that it was a mistake to get involved. But how could I not? It was my job.

Laurel swallowed and slid the glass across the table toward me. "Would you become free too?"

I didn't answer, because I didn't have to. I was sucking down ice cream, and she was already posing another question. "I'm asking because I don't think my father has long and then…" She looked down at the table, her expression torn. After several beats her eyes met mine. "And then when would we see each other?"

I understood her desperation. It's hard for the living to put their lives on hold for the dying. "We'd make time."

Laurel looked disappointed, like maybe she wanted to cry. She made it clear that I'd given her the wrong answer. "It just kills me to see him suffer. I feel so helpless. And the truth is, Max, I've never been very good at that."

She had mentioned this many times before. But this time there was something else in her, something she was holding back, something that was trying to find its way out. Finally, it did. "Can't we help him along? I mean, surely there must be something we can do."

"Physician-assisted suicide is illegal," I explained.

"Illegal, maybe," she quipped. "But what about ethically? Morally? I'd euthanize a dog for less."

I didn't offer a response.

She kept at me. "Surely you can see that."

"It's complicated."

"I used to work in pharma," she scoffed. "Nothing is that complicated."

"Laurel?"

She and I both looked up at the same time.

"James!" she exclaimed, her brows shooting toward the ceiling.

I didn't recognize the man towering over us, but I could take a pretty good guess at who it was.

# CHAPTER TWENTY-SIX

Laurel Dunaway

Journal Entry

I did my best to act casual. The main thing, or so I've heard, is to make it look as though you don't feel guilty. I've yet to decide whether or not this is true. Whatever the case, if James is upset with me, so far, he isn't letting it show.

After he arrived home from work, he showered and suggested we go out for dinner. Nothing out of the ordinary about that.

He was his usual self over dinner: attentive, calm, perhaps a bit stoic. He asked about Dad, but he did not bring up Max Hastings.

I was careful to steer clear of all of the typical landmines. Ever since the incident at the office, and the situation with the cat, speaking about anything that really matters has all but ceased. I swore that I didn't hurt Leo—I wouldn't—*couldn't*. But the fact that I lied about the missing food, James said, puts doubt in his mind. He can't help himself.

Thankfully, his choice of hire has allowed me a bit of leeway. He's angry with me, but also just enough in the wrong that he can't dole out the punishment he's not yet sure I deserve.

Over dinner, I questioned him about work. He filled me in on where things stand, in terms of user data and sales figures. Our love language. Listening to him speak, hearing the details of his day, gave me a slight rush. The truth is I miss it. I miss being at the office, in the thick of it, instead of banished to the outskirts. It's not easy to wash something out of your system. Especially when you've given that something blood, sweat, and tears for nearly a decade.

The rush did not go unnoticed by my husband. The fact that we were business partners before we were lovers means we understand each other in a way we might not otherwise.

We hadn't meant to sleep together, James and I. It was a mistake. We said we wouldn't mix business with pleasure. We tried to keep those promises. Turned out, it only added fuel to the fire. The rest of it was a natural progression, you could say.

When we met, when we agreed to the business partnership, we had both been involved with other people. Neither of us were married. But we weren't single, either. James likes to say it was a gray area. Either way, seventy- and eighty-hour work-weeks took care of the relationship-with-other-people issue real fast.

He smiled over his salad, noting the flush of my cheeks. He sensed my anxiety in the way I leaned in. I know this because he said, after sipping his glass of red, "Work isn't going anywhere. You know that. Take the time, Laurel. You need it."

"I miss it," I replied, slicing into my filet. My eyes met his. "Although, you're right. I have been a bit of a disaster."

"You have a lot on your plate. It's understandable."

"Is it though?" I asked a little too loudly for his liking. Heads raised, eyes turned in our direction. My question, the extra attention, and the subsequent dig was just the kind of backhanded compliment my husband hates. "I don't recall you being so under-standing when you hired her."

He lowered his voice to a whisper, speaking through gritted teeth. "She has working knowledge of the company. You know how close we are to selling. And *you* of all people should know how important it is that our numbers look good. Especially now."

"I was handling it."

His jaw tightened. James does not like confrontation. He does not like to be questioned. "Not like it needs to be handled."

"Says who?"

"Says me." I looked on as he downed his glass of wine before speaking.

"I'm not sure what kind of fantasy world you're living in, Laurel—but we can't just let everything we've worked for go to shit just because your dad got sick."

I scoff because there's so much to unpack in what he's said. "I just don't understand why didn't you discuss it with me?"

"I didn't think it would be such a big deal."

"You're not that stupid."

"Laurel," he said firmly, pinning me with his eyes before pulling my wineglass toward his side of the table. "We're going to enjoy ourselves tonight."

I took a stab at the piece of meat, smiled, and forced it into my mouth.

IT STARTED WITH THE CAT AND SNOWBALLED FROM THERE. Although, now that I think of it, it was before the cat.

Months ago, there were the two flat tires. I hadn't thought much of it at the time. Neighborhood kids. Back then, I didn't have much of a reason than to think it was anything other than an isolated incident...an inconvenience.

But then, last week I found the word "bitch" etched into the hood of my car. It was there, permanently, like a warning. James promised we'd get cameras installed. Catch the little prankster red handed. So far he hasn't gotten around to it.

This week started with incessant phone calls from a blocked number. Telemarketers are boundless, James said when I showed him my phone. Just change your settings, he told me, as though I hadn't thought of that. As though that was the point.

Yesterday, it got worse. Yesterday, there was a dead bird on my windshield. It was awful, splayed out like whoever put it there wanted to send a message.

And then, last night, at dinner, it came when a message was delivered to our table. Origami, folded in the shape of a bird. I will admit that when I unfolded it, it gave me a sense of justification. Now my husband would see that I'm not paranoid, and I'm not crazy. Neighborhood kids wouldn't go so far as to follow us to a restaurant downtown.

James laughed it off. Well, he didn't actually think it was funny. "There are some lonely people in this world," he'd said. "It's probably just someone who saw a beautiful woman and wanted her to know she's being noticed."

I unfolded the bird, knowing with everything in me, all the way to the marrow of my bones, that it was more than that. Words written in red jumped out at me. *You next.*

I held it up so he could see. "You don't think it's an odd thing to write?"

"It's strange," he quipped. "But it's paper, Laurel—how harmful could it be?"

I recanted the story about finding the bird on my windshield.

"A coincidence, I'm sure." He seemed almost amused. James gets off on seeing me one step beyond the edge, so I shouldn't have been surprised "Sometimes," he said, "I think you read a little too much into things."

But I'm not so sure.

~

THE FIRST THING I NOTICED AS WE TURNED INTO OUR DRIVE WAS how dark it was. James accused me of forgetting to turn on the outside lights, even though I knew I had. "This is not good," I said. "I don't think we should go inside."

"Tell you what," he replied with one of his reassuring smiles. "You stay put. I'll go in and make sure everything is all right."

"I don't think—"

"I'll text you." He was already half out the door. I wanted to jump out of the car; whether it was to stop him or follow him, I wasn't sure. Halfway up the drive he pressed the remote, locking the car doors. He flexed his muscles as though to say, *I got this.*

If this were a horror flick, this would be the part where the very stupid yet chivalrous man walks into something that ends up getting him killed.

But this is not a horror flick, lucky for my husband. And lucky for me.

*Just a blown fuse,* James texts after an eternity. It's not that I believed him—just that I couldn't very well camp out in the car. I saw it differently. I saw it for what it was. A bad omen.

*I'll come walk you in.*

My husband always liked playing the hero. So I let him. It keeps life on an even keel.

Once inside, I double-and then triple-checked the doors, ensuring they were locked. James kissed my forehead and told me I needed to rest. He assured me that he'd checked everything. He promised he'd get the lights changed out in the morning. "Go to bed," he said. "I'll come up and join you in a second." He had work to do in the office. He wanted to email our handyman to make sure he'd be able to come by tomorrow to replace the fuses.

It was well past midnight before he finally came to bed. He kissed my cheek and called it a night. Only one of us slept. When I was certain that he'd properly drifted off, I found myself tiptoeing through the house, logging onto his laptop. Before I knew it, I was clicking through his emails. I scanned his texts for good measure. I don't know that I have anything to worry about. But I don't know that I *don't* either.

He's been stressed about the sale of our company. We're both ready to move on, and now it's time to cash in on what we built so that we can do that. My husband, however, is holding out, while I think the offer on the table is good enough.

Maybe I shouldn't have been snooping. Although, how else am I supposed to stay privy to what's going on? This way, it makes it easy to slip suggestions in through normal, everyday conversation. I found a few things nestled in his inbox that warranted a conversation. But nothing of significance.

It wasn't until I dug into the project management app our company uses to communicate deadlines and such that I found something of real interest. It was a message between him and one of our attorneys.

*I think Laurel is having an affair. You know what this means...*

I should have stopped there. I panicked, instead. The important thing in any crisis is not to react until you've thought things through. You have to weigh your options and develop a strategy from there. That's not what I did. Not really. And once a thing is done, what can you do?

# CHAPTER TWENTY-SEVEN

Dr. Max Hastings

AFTER

D r. Jones stared at me furtively. "Well?"

I rolled my neck. My shoulders had grown stiff from so much sitting. The mattresses in this place leave a lot to be desired. Not that it matters. Sleep remains pretty much nonexistent. But that wasn't why I was stretching. I was stalling. I don't like recalling that day.

She pressed onward. "What did he say? James Dunaway? In the diner..."

"He said nothing."

As usual, it was Laurel who did most of the talking. "James"—I recall the way she motioned, widely—"You remember Dr. Hastings?"

I extended my hand. "Max."

"Dr. Hastings—*Max*—is treating my father."

"Right." He seemed to be searching his mind, looking for something misplaced. We shook hands. His grip was firm but friendly, which is to say it gave nothing away. "A physician," he remarked with a jutted lip, "The Lord's work."

"Dr. Hastings," Laurel said, plentiful with the formalities, "Thinks Dad could benefit from a feeding tube. But I think…" Her brow furrowed, and she paused as though she'd just recalled something long forgotten. "Wait. What are you doing here?"

"I had a meeting a few blocks over."

I watched the two of them. James Dunaway scooted into the booth next to me, across from his wife. He glanced sideways in my direction. "Never tried this place. Thought I'd check it out." He paused, looked toward the counter, and then directly over at me. "And now I have."

Dr. Jones narrowed her eyes. "You weren't worried?"

"Not really."

"How did he seem?"

"He didn't seem like anything."

I pictured James Dunaway now, with his ashen complexion and the eternally grumpy expression that appeared to be plastered on his face. I wondered what he knew. I wondered who might have told him.

"Did you think he knew?"

"Up until that moment, no. No one knew about our affair. We were careful—we were discreet."

"Who do you think could have told him? Your brother? Nina? Mrs. Dunaway's father?"

I smiled at her line of questioning.

"There's still someone…" she remarked, very much leading the witness.

My head cocked to the side. "Who?"

"Max. Come on. Can't you see? Remember what you said last week?"

I averted my gaze. My mind followed where my heart dared not go.

"It isn't possible that Laurel—"

"No."

"Why not?"

I didn't respond. The answer to that question still lay far ahead.

For the moment, I saw myself easing out of that diner booth, excusing myself politely but hastily. As it was, Ellie would be waiting for me. She never forgot a promise to take her for a swim, and she expected me to be punctual.

As I slid behind the wheel of my sedan, I recalled exactly what I'd been thinking that afternoon. I was thinking that I'd fucked up. I was thinking that I'd gotten too close. I'd crossed a line that maybe I shouldn't have crossed. The first rule of any love affair, I knew well. Never get involved with someone who has less to lose than you do. Laurel, it appeared, did not have so very much to lose.

The realization made my stomach choppy. But then, it could have been the ice cream. Just a half hour earlier, I had felt at one with the entire world. How could I describe the deep heaviness that had washed over me? It wasn't fear. At the time, I had no reason to suspect anything was catastrophically wrong.

Dr. Jones looked perplexed. "It strikes me as odd that you wouldn't have reacted after the incident at the diner. I know if it were my wife…it wouldn't have gone down quite calmly. Which will make it hard to prove James Dunaway was certain of the affair. We'll need a way to explain this to the jury…"

She makes a good point. *I wasn't thinking about that at the time. I was mostly thinking that I'd put my job in jeopardy.*

To avoid the freeway, I had taken the long way home, winding through the city. The afternoon was slowly fading, but the heat of the day radiated off the pavement, creating a mirage. I passed the care home, and the park across the street, and finally the coffee shop a few blocks down.

In November of the previous year, it was there that it had all began. I wondered, if I could go back in time, if I might have done things differently.

# CHAPTER TWENTY-EIGHT

Laurel Dunaway

Journal Entry

I've been thinking a lot about writing my life story, with some of the inconsequential parts taken out. Dr. Miller says I could write it as a novel or a screenplay—that either would do. The point is just to get it out. Sometimes after James is asleep, I take my notebook down to the living room, put on a pot of tea, and I write. Usually I write about grown-up me, present day stuff, but Dr. Miller asked me to write from the perspective of my younger self. It seemed weird when I first tried it. But Dr. Miller taught me something. She taught me the importance of backstory. She says it's easy to predict the future once you can clearly see the past. She says that most people can't, and that's why so many of us just end up repeating the same mistakes.

∾

THE LITTLE GIRL SWIMS. SHE SWIMS AND SHE SWIMS. FOR TWENTY-six hours, she is later told, the little girl hid in the woods. She was afraid to come out because of the mommy. The mommy called for the girl, the little girl swears, even though the daddy tells her, mostly at night when she can't sleep, that it isn't possible.

Divers searched the lake. The little girl was presumed dead, until she was found on a rural road, very much alive.

A nice lady explained to the little girl that the mommy couldn't hurt her. She'd gone to heaven.

Overnight the little girl became a star. She was thrust into the spotlight. Her picture and her story were everywhere. She became a household name. It was a miracle she was alive. Donations poured in from all over the country. Some even from other countries. Places the little girl had yet to hear of. Even now, people still send gifts to her father's address on her birthday.

Everyone said the fact that the little girl survived had to be ordained by God. The little girl is proof that miracles can happen. Who doesn't want a miracle? Who doesn't want to believe? She gave them a reason. She gave them hope. Her life became evidence that God and angels and all things holy exist.

The little girl liked the attention. It made her feel not so sad, like maybe there were nice people in the world. Like maybe there were mommies in the world who care. Just not hers. She liked being special. But deep down, she always knew the truth: what had really saved her that night was that when worse came to worse, she'd learned how to swim.

# CHAPTER TWENTY-NINE

Dr. Max Hastings

AFTER

"Do you ever recall Laurel being upset with you…did you ever give her cause to say…want to get back at you?"

"How do you mean?"

"I'm asking if she seemed upset with you, especially toward the end?"

"Upset?"

"Yeah…you know…bitter. Resentful. You know how women can be." Dr. Jones posed the same tired questions, even though we'd been over this. I assume my attorney hired her because she's good, but I'll admit, she's a bit of a bore. She has a low opinion of women, and it showed.

"I don't think so."

"How do you know for sure?"

"She thanked me once," I told her. I pictured Laurel all those months ago. She had seemed to mean it. She said finding me again had been one of the best things to ever happen to her. She looked humble when she'd said it, if not a bit shy, almost like a little girl.

"I've wanted this for forever," she said.

I didn't think much of it. Forever could mean a lot of things. It could have meant since last week, or since yesterday afternoon. But then she clarified things when she said, "You remember that big girl...the one with the birthmark on her face?"

"Who?"

"I think her name was..." Her nose was twisted up toward her brow in the funny little way it did when she was unsure. "God, I can't recall."

"Lisa?"

She shrugged. "You dated her for months."

"Yeah, that was Lisa. You have a good memory," I told her. Lisa became a dermatologist, which made sense. She was smart, *very* smart, and that birthmark wasn't a birthmark, it was psoriasis.

"Not really," Laurel countered. "Anyway—I think I saw you together once. At a Christmas party...maybe...? Anyway, you must have been about sixteen..."

"At the Weatherfords. We had sex in the bathroom."

She seemed surprised. "You remember the party?"

The truth was I didn't really recall Laurel back then. However, to have said as much seemed like it would be an insult. At the time, I had only been focused on two things: going pre-med and getting laid.

My brow rose. "I remember because it was my first time."

"For her as well?"

"I don't know. I didn't have enough experience back then to notice that."

She turned further toward me until her naked belly rested on mine. "Well, I hated her."

"Really?"

"Yeah, for months, I thought of ways to make her suffer."

"And did you find any?"

"No, I settled on hoping it would happen by accident."

Dr. Jones listens as I recant the story, but she doesn't seem that interested. Her expression tells me she's already in the process of changing her line of questioning. This is a thing I've noticed with people. They lack stamina. They're always flitting from one thing to the next, without giving any particular thing too much thought. I suppose I, too, was in the habit of that once. "Would you say Nina was a good wife?"

"She was my first and only, so who's to say?"

"But she took care of your daughter?"

"Yes."

"And she was good at home? She enjoyed domestic life?"

"She worked too. I can't say whether she enjoyed it, but yes, she did the lion's share of work at home."

"Is that why you married her?"

"When I married her, I had no way of knowing what kind of wife or mother she'd be."

"Why did you marry her?"

"Because she was intelligent."

"Intelligent..."

"I assumed that she would offer good genetic material. And she was a hard worker."

She narrows her gaze. "Is that all?"

I shrug.

"So you had no reason to be disgruntled with her?"

How could I answer that in a way that made sense? "No," I said, even though it wasn't entirely true. What married person doesn't have a reason to be disgruntled, at least on occasion? How can it be possible to entangle your entire life with another person and not in some small way find fault from time to time?

"So the afternoon you ran into James Dunaway at the diner... do you recall what it was that had frightened you?"

I thought back to that evening, back to the drive home. I

considered what might have unsettled me. Everything. Nothing in particular. Although, it was pretty obvious that the odds of it being an accident that James stumbled upon us in that diner were pretty slim. "I don't know."

"Did you consider James Dunaway to be a violent man?"

"I didn't really know James. But I was sleeping with his wife, so you can surmise what you will from my behavior."

"Did you consider that he might be armed?"

"No."

"It never crossed your mind."

"I figured if he wanted me dead, I wouldn't have left the diner."

"Were you afraid for your family?"

I didn't know how to answer that. More importantly, I hardly know how it matters anyhow. Considering the circumstances.

The thought made me anxious, even now. I stood and sort of shuffled around, to the extent that I could. I balled and then flexed my cuffed hands. My ankles are shackled, so I can only sort of wobble, and not far from the table. I am desperate for air. I am desperate to breathe. This relentless barrage of questions is growing old. I long for the past, when no one seemed particularly concerned with my comings and goings. My private life was just that. Private.

It's hard to appreciate simplicity until it is taken away. And life had been just that, simple. I was a doctor. I treated patients. I was a husband and a father. I went to work, and I came home. I took my daughter to swim therapy. I dug around a little in the garden whenever I found the time. Sometimes I played racquetball with my brother. It was a rather ordinary life.

But first with the police, and then the detectives, followed by my lawyer, and now by Dr. Jones, that has all changed. When I appeared in court, in front of the judge initially, back when I was denied bail, I had been delivered to the court in an unmarked car so as not to tip off the press. It was pointless, in the end. The media swarmed like flies around a pile of shit on a hot day.

In fact, they are still swarming. I have become a pariah— my story something to be broken down and consumed, sold in bite-sized bits.

It will not end, this I know—not until this case grows cold, goes stale, until there's a bigger tragedy they can leech onto.

"After you arrived home, from the diner, what happened then?"

"Nina had ordered delivery service."

"Takeout?"

"Yes. She had ordered from the menu at Sullivan's."

"Sullivan's. That was important how?"

"It's the place I took her every year on our anniversary."

"And?"

"She said she just felt like eating it."

*"And?"*

"And I didn't mind."

"You didn't think it was a bit odd?"

"I was preoccupied. My mind had been on other things. I was aware it wasn't our anniversary. But other than that, I didn't give my wife's dinner choice much thought."

"Then what?"

"Then we ate. I took my daughter to swim therapy. Afterward, I watched her in the bath and put her to bed."

"After that?"

"After that, I went to work in my office."

"Was it normal for you to work at night?"

"It wasn't abnormal. I had some charting I needed to finish up."

"And did you do the charting?"

"Yes," I tell her, which is the truth. "But it was about that time that I felt a sense of sheer panic. Not unease, like what had happened after the incident at the diner. This was worse. It was gut-wrenching sorrow. I broke out in a cold sweat until I was forced to get up from my desk and crack a window. When I went back to my charts, my hands shook. I felt dizzy."

"A premonition?" she questioned.

"I don't know."

"Sounds to me like a panic attack."

"Maybe."

"That had never happened to you prior?"

"Not in a long time."

"Is that why you told your wife you had to see about a patient?"

"Partly."

"And then you drove by the Dunaway place?"

"Yes."

"Did anything seem suspicious? Out of the ordinary?"

"I didn't know what to expect. So, no."

"You'd never driven by before?"

"I don't think so."

"Did you have the feeling that after the encounter at the diner that you'd lost her?"

"Who? Laurel?" I asked, confused. I hadn't thought of it that way.

"You'd been involved for months in a heady affair."

This is not how I would describe Laurel and I at all. The term 'heady affair' reduced what happened between us as something illicit, no more than a passing fancy. By the time I drove by her house, I'd suspected it was more than that. I was pretty sure for the both of us.

# CHAPTER THIRTY

Laurel Dunaway

Journal Entry

It was after two in the morning when I woke James to tell him I'd gotten the call. Dad was not well. His breathing was labored. He was asking for me. I had to go.

Most of this, of course, was a lie.

Or rather, what I like to call a projection of the future.

Some people stand by and wait for life to happen to them. Then there are people like me, who refuse to accept the status quo. It's possible to create your reality, and I was well on my way to do just that.

As I stood at Dad's bedside, I whispered my goodbyes. I told him that it was time for him to go. That it was okay. That it was time for the both of us. Then I held the pillow over his face and leaned all of me into it. As far as deaths go, it would be quick and painless. How much more can a person ask for?

I knew that Max would have ordered something to help Dad sleep. I'd asked him to do it. Which meant that I also knew that it would be easy to suffocate him. He wouldn't—or rather he couldn't—put up much of a fight.

If my husband asked for the details, I would tell him the truth. Which version of it, well, it depends on how you look at it. After all, what is truth but perception?

Care homes are often run by well-meaning people. People who also happen to be overworked and underpaid. Sometimes not very educated either.

Which is how I knew that no one would question Dad's death. Like me, they too were all pretty sick of dealing with him. He was just one patient among many. He was a tick mark on a long list of to-do's. Something to be checked off. Something to be dealt with. At any rate, there was a revolving door of new problems to deal with. His bed would not remain empty for long. A welcome, albeit short-lived, vacancy. It was no skin off of their back.

Thankfully, I was not wrong.

# CHAPTER THIRTY-ONE

Dr. Max Hastings

AFTER

"You mentioned something last time," Dr. Jones said. "Something I hadn't given much thought until...until now."

I wasn't sure what she was going to say. But I was aware of one thing. She is not the quitting kind. This makes her a damn fine psychiatrist and, at the same time, a thorn in my side.

"Your daughter...you mentioned swim therapy."

"That's right."

"What kind of therapy?"

"She's autistic."

"Autistic." Her eyes widened. "Jesus, Max. Why didn't you mention this earlier?"

"I don't see how it relates."

"It gives us something...God." She paused and then shook her head. "How could I not see this?" I shifted under the weight of her gaze. "I really wish you would have said something, Max," she said, indignantly. "Why didn't you say anything?"

I hadn't volunteered the information, because it's not my daughter who has been accused of anything.

"Max," she said in that brisk, arrogant way she excelled at. "It's almost like you don't care about your freedom."

"I didn't see how it was relevant," I told her, which isn't entirely true.

"Your wife didn't take this particularly well?"

"How do you mean?"

"She developed a bit of a habit, you might say?"

"It depends."

"Depends on what?"

"Your definition of a habit."

"The drinking. The colleague of Nina's you mentioned to me... she mentioned Nina would sometimes show up for work with liquor on her breath."

I stared at the floor. Suddenly, I became acutely aware of all the noises inside and outside of me, like an orchestra tuning up to play. The rapid thump of my heart, the blood beating in my ears. The dizzy feeling came on strong. There's something to be said for a man that knows he's about to come face to face with his own faults. It's not pretty.

"When did the drinking start?"

"I don't know."

"Are we talking years or months? Weeks?"

*Years*, I think but don't say. I certainly hadn't known Nina had a drinking problem. I hadn't known a lot of things, it turned out. The saddest part...I hadn't even suspected.

I had been working a lot, and sure, partaking in vices of my own. Nevertheless, there are certain things a man should know about his wife. A doctor, a good one, should have noticed such issues, shouldn't he? That's what Dr. Jones is thinking. It's written all over her face.

Maybe she's right. Maybe I was ignorant. Or maybe Nina was just very good at hiding the things she did not want anyone to see.

In hindsight, those were the wrong questions to ask. And anyhow, the truth always seems to have a way of coming out.

～

IT WAS APPARENT FROM THE BEGINNING THAT ELLIE WASN'T normal. She didn't cry straightaway, and then not even when they poked her, rolling the needle around, trying to manipulate her tiny veins, each time, failing. I wanted to push everyone aside and start the IV myself. I wanted to fix her. I knew then, just as I know now, that some things that are broken cannot be fixed.

It didn't stop me from trying.

Meeting my daughter had not turned out to be the joyous occasion I'd envisioned. It was the first time in my life I can ever recall feeling truly helpless.

Her Apgar Score was low. She was listless, ashen, and of all of the physicians in the room, including myself, no one except for my wife knew what was wrong. I've been scared since, terribly scared, but I've never been as scared as I was in that moment.

"You hadn't known that your wife had consumed alcohol during the pregnancy?" the neonatologist questioned.

"No."

The alcohol was a shame, one that Nina was forced to admit when it came down to it. But even I had reservations about it being the catalyst that caused my daughter's condition.

"Why didn't you leave her?" Dr. Jones would later ask.

It was a question I had asked of myself any number of times.

It was a question with a very clear-cut, unclear answer. How could I leave my wife? What would leaving solve in the context of where we were with an infant who had more needs than either of us had planned on? Sure, I probably could have won custody. But what then? Nina wasn't going to just fade into the background. I knew that much about her. But most of all, the thing about a sudden betrayal, the thing you can't know until you're in the thick of it, is it doesn't allow for much room to move.

~

THE NIGHT NINA ORDERED TAKEOUT FROM SULLIVAN'S, THE NIGHT I left to drive by Laurel's house, something else unsettling had happened. Something I hadn't told my attorney and certainly not Dr. Jones.

Nina had informed me that she'd found a place for Ellie. She'd placed a deposit, and she wanted us to go and visit the following weekend. She'd scheduled a tour. It didn't come as much of a shock as the drinking, but it wasn't entirely expected either. Ellie had been doing good. She was showing improvement. Slowly, sure. But improvement, nonetheless.

Ever since the official diagnosis, we'd worked hard to come up with a treatment plan that would allow her to thrive. There were far more options than I'd had as a kid—not that I'd ever been diagnosed. The medical community hardly understood spectrum disorders back then, unless you were on the far end. Which I wasn't. Not like Ellie.

"We can always have another, Max."

All sensory input became intensified. Clearly, she'd given this a lot more thought than I'd realized. Nina was well aware that I'd had a vasectomy three months after Ellie's birth. She was also well aware there were other ways.

Even though I don't think she meant it about having another baby, I told her our daughter was enough, for the both of us. I told her in no uncertain terms that I was not interested in having another child

"You're right," she'd whispered later in the dark. "I'm sorry. I shouldn't have brought it up. It's just sometimes I wonder what it would be like, don't you? To have a normal life?"

I didn't answer my wife. The truth is I was afraid. I was afraid that I might slip, and if I did, years of pent up rage might escape. I was afraid I would do something that I could never, ever take back.

But Nina didn't stop there. "I've been thinking...before summer is over...before we get her settled in at the facility... that I should take her up to the mountains. Santa Fe...*Colorado*, maybe. I think a change of scenery and some cooler air would do her good."

"I'll come too," I said, in a thin voice that hardly resembled my own. The words came out so fast I didn't have a chance at a second thought. Looking back, I chalk it up to the exhaustion. After the day I'd had, fresh mountain air hadn't sounded like a half-bad idea. Escaping the heat seemed like a no-brainer, once the idea had been presented and was out in the open. More than anything, I thought it would buy me time. Time to convince my wife. Time to come up with another plan.

Nina turned to me in the dark. "When would we leave?"

"I'll need to get someone to cover my cases...but it shouldn't be too difficult."

"You think your associates will go for it?" She sounded hopeful, and I realized maybe this was what she wanted all along—some help. A little give out of me.

"I don't know. But they can't say much...I have the vacation time."

"So in a few days then?"

I offered a conciliatory smile I was aware she couldn't see. "Most likely in a few days. By the weekend, if I can swing it."

# CHAPTER THIRTY-TWO

Laurel Dunaway

Journal Entry

The little girl feels a sharp pain in her chest, like a knife stabbing her. This is a different pain than the one she felt in the water. It's suffocating, but it takes longer. She's afraid as she lies in the dark, too scared to pull the cover up over her head, too scared not to. Her eyes stay fixed on the light underneath her bedroom door. She watches for the shifting of light. She listens for footsteps. She hadn't realized she could be any more afraid than when her mommy put her in the water, but now she knows she can. She hears the doorknob turning, feels the weight of him stepping into the room.

"Sammy?" the daddy calls. Back then, the girl answered to a different name. "Sammy, I can't sleep..."

That made two of them.

The girl dared not answer the daddy. She knew better. It was worse if he knew she was awake. "I'm sad, darling. Are you sad?" The daddy lifted the covers and crawled into the twin-sized bed. The little girl curled into a ball. "It's okay," he said, soothingly. "You don't have to be scared."

The daddy's tears soaked through the little girl's nightgown. It was as though a tidal wave had broken through a poorly designed dam. He pulled her close, sobs shaking the bed like an earthquake. He went on crying in hard violent bursts. It wasn't until he was done that the really scary stuff began. She wondered if it was possible for a person to cry themselves to death. She hoped it was. A crack ran down her bedroom wall. The little girl remembered the mommy telling the daddy to fix it. He never did, and now she was glad. It gave her something to focus on when the daddy slipped into her bed. She imagined herself shrinking, shrinking so small, small enough so that she could squeeze through the crack. She imagined other worlds on the other side, entire universes where mommies and daddies didn't hurt their children. Where mommies didn't die and daddies never cried. "Thank God," he said at last, when the force of his crying trailed off some. "She can't hurt us anymore."

～

DR. MILLER WANTS ME TO TALK ABOUT MY FATHER'S DEATH IN WAYS that I can't. She says it's important that I find an outlet for my grief. If only I could explain the extent of it. If only she knew how very deep it ran.

Then, later, when James advised me to put on something special, I saw it for what it was: an outlet for my grief. The only one currently at my disposal.

As usual, he was the one to set the appointment. But this time was different. There was no unease, no fear; there was nothing, just blank space between my ears and a feeling that I would let it lead me where it would.

If anything, I felt more unease about potentially being left alone. With the creepy stuff and with Dad gone, I was eager for things to return to normal.

I had thought that I'd be anxious to get back to work. But even that moved too slowly to really offer much of a challenge. It didn't have an edge like the care home, where things were literally life and death. It didn't hold the same excitement, the kind I'd found on the inside of the affair with Max.

Since Dad's death, I no longer have an excuse to see him. Knowing that my husband is suspicious means I'm not sure I really want one. Dr. Miller suggested the end of the affair only adds to the grief. She said that if I don't find a healthy way to deal with my emotions that it's possible things could get really bad. Dr. Miller doesn't understand I have coping methods for days.

"We have to hurry," James said suddenly, his way of informing me of the party. He left a period of silence afterward that allowed his words to take me back to the beginning, to the people we were when we fell in love. Dr. Miller had questioned me about this during our last session, suggesting that maybe one—or both—of us had outgrown the marriage. It's possible, I'd told her. She said grief changes a person. It makes life seem more imminent. I don't know if this is true. Looking at my husband now, it's clear. We're the same as we ever were in some ways, but also radically different.

"What do you think?" I asked holding up a few dresses for him to choose from, full well knowing which it would be.

He appeared to mull it over, fooling no one but himself with his deliberation. Finally, he pointed to the little black dress, the one with all the memories. "Definitely that one."

By the time I was finished getting ready, I had transformed from sad Laurel into more of whom I was once, the hotheaded girl with big dreams and intoxicating power. I found James waiting by the door, a book of poetry in his hand. *Nietzsche.* No doubt recommended by someone he met. Maybe *she'd* even mentioned it, and my husband, being the kind of man he is, took a simple suggestion and decided to become an expert. Like most things with him, it was all for show.

~

I CAN'T SAY WHAT I'D BEEN THINKING ABOUT DURING THE DRIVE, only that my mind was clear, for the first time in a long time. I hadn't even thought much about where we were going, not until he pulled in the parking garage.

"Here?" I asked, my stomach convulsing.

"Is there something wrong?"

I shook my head slowly. "We never meet at hotels."

James snorted. "Always and never are seldom correct..."

He placed his hand on mine after killing the ignition. "There's no reason to be nervous, love. When have I ever let you down?"

I didn't say anything more. I simply followed him up the stairwell, down the hall, and straight into Room 553.

~

SHE WASN'T THE FIRST WOMAN MY HUSBAND TOOK THINGS TOO FAR with. I was thinking about the first as he closed the door. "So," he said, donning his most appealing Cheshire cat grin. "There's something I need to tell you."

My eyes scanned the room. This was a party, all right. His mistress sat cross-legged on the bed.

I swallowed hard. Not because I was nervous—I was too familiar with this game. The big reveal. His biggest yet. "You remember Nina?"

My eyes shifted from my husband to her. Her eyes remained on him. She wasn't even gutsy enough to look me in the eye.

"Nina and I have been seeing each other," he exclaimed. "And we thought that you should know." He said it like he didn't know that I already knew, because that is the thing about my husband, he is an expert liar.

"I'm sorry," Nina lamented. "We didn't mean for anyone to get hurt."

"But someone always gets hurt, though, don't they?" I remarked, directing my attention to my husband.

He smiled in a sad kind of way. "There's just one thing I don't understand, Laurel..."

"What's that?"

"Why you had to go and fuck Max Hastings."

"You know how it is," I said. "An eye for an eye."

His mistress looked confused. She laughed it off at first, a nervous kind of laugh, the kind that gave away the fact that the joke was on her. "Max? You're fucking Max?"

"In that very bed," I told her with a nod. "All over this room, really."

Her gaze sharply fell to the floor. She recovered quickly, kind of shrugging like she didn't care, although it was very obvious that she did. No one likes being betrayed, especially if they're quite good at it themselves.

But it was more than that. Nina was not a stupid woman. If she had been, she would not have been able to weasel her way into my life and so thoroughly into my business. The wheels had begun turning in her mind. She was wondering, given that I was fucking her husband, if that was the sole reason mine was fucking her.

The problem with that line of thinking is that it wasn't the point.

"Well, darling," James said. "Now that everything is good and properly out in the open, what do you suppose we do now?"

I looked to Nina and then back at James. "Now, you do what you do."

WHY JAMES INITIALLY LIED TO ME ABOUT NINA HASTINGS I WASN'T sure. All I knew was that if I wanted to protect everything I held dear, there was only one thing I could do. Strike preemptively.

"Did you bring the rest?" he asked, sliding into his favorite pair of gloves. He wore them a lot this past winter, and I tried to tell him not to get too attached. Not everything is built to last. It was a sentiment that only two people long married, two people who understood the other's strengths and weaknesses, maybe better than their own, could offer. He smiled and said he was just breaking them in.

I couldn't see it at the time. Maybe I didn't want to see it. I'm good at lying, best when it comes to lying to myself. Hindsight is twenty-twenty. He wasn't trying to prove a point. He was trying to raise the stakes. "I'll get you a new pair for Christmas," I'd said, using the power of suggestion.

He told me there was no need; winter wouldn't last forever. That's my husband, always speaking in code.

It's also how I knew this one was a problem. She wasn't going to go away as easy as the rest.

"Laurel—the stuff," he demands. "Did you bring it?"

Things move in slow motion when you get to the end, so it takes me several beats before I answer him. "Of course I did."

He was on her before I finished my sentence. That fire in his eyes, the hunger I've so rarely seen over the last few months, was lit and burning bright. Even though I could have done without the drama, just to see its return is surely worth it. "What about the rest of it?" he asked, landing a blow to her temple. "Tell me you didn't forget."

"Well, it's not like you told me it was going to be tonight." I was toying with him, of course. Any time James mentions an appointment, I make sure I'm prepared. After that first time, it would be a mistake not to.

I retrieve the items from my bag and hold them up. He grinned. "God, Laurel. What would I do without you?"

I smiled because he knows me so well. Over the months, I'd collected things from Max. A belt. A tie. A pocketknife. Little things. Mementos. Things he should have noticed but didn't. I suppose it's easy to flee without all of your belongings when the woman you're having a fling with suddenly starts pressuring you for more. I was almost disappointed. Max was such a thorough kind of guy. Although, I can speak from experience, it's normal to be a little distracted when you have injuries you have to contend with. Injuries you're worried about having to explain away.

I watched as James wrapped Max's belt around her neck and pulled, pulled, pulled. First her lips turn blue and then the rest of her face.

Eventually—this part never takes as long as I want it to— she passes out. It turns me on, the way my husband tied her wrists to the bed using Max's ties. He uses that new knot he spoke of months ago; I know because it's one I've never seen. It's amazing how things come full circle.

"Do you want to do the honors?" James asked, once she was proudly splayed on the bed. That's always been his favorite part, the set up.

"No."

He nodded his gratitude. "I'm sorry, Laurel. I know this took a little longer than you wanted." He looked remorseful. Almost sullen. "But you know I could never love another woman the way I love you."

"I know."

"She didn't mean anything to me."

"I know."

He studied her carefully. I could see he was committing her to memory. Sometimes I think that's where all the good stuff lies, in the past.

"It was you with the bird, wasn't it?"

"No," he said.

It was a test, and I was grateful he'd passed. It couldn't have been him. Because it was me—with the bird and with the cat and with all the rest. What I really needed was a good story, something that would sell. Something that would make sense for a man as meticulous as Max Hastings.

"I'm going to miss her," James remarked. "She was one of the crazier ones, for sure."

"Is she dead?"

He looked over at me. Sweat beaded at his brow. He checked her pulse. "Almost."

"It's time to put this to bed."

He sighed heavily. He wasn't ready for it to be over. He wanted to delay the rush.

I checked the time. "James."

Finally, he gripped Max's belt, cupped his gloved hand over her face, and gave it his all. I don't know that I'll ever not think of that belt and feel some sense of satisfaction. It represented endurance and stamina. The ability to hang in there. All things one needs in a marriage. Sadly, though, not for Nina Hastings. I don't mean to make it sound like she didn't put up a good fight. She really, really did.

# CHAPTER THIRTY-THREE

Dr. Max Hastings

AFTER

"I think we should talk more about that night."

I don't have to ask Dr. Jones which of them she is referring to. I know. This is the way she works. Forward and backward, winding this way and that way, any way she can, to try and trip me up. Her, with her patronizing glare and her ever-assessing nature. I understood this. Not so long ago, I lived out my days this way too. Always evaluating, making endless judgment calls.

"The night your wife was murdered. Let's go back there," she said, making it personal. She crossed and uncrossed her legs, only to cross them again. "You went home after work?" she asked, chewing at her pencil, like a dog onto a scent, relentless and unmovable. "Briefly."

"Nina had texted me and asked me to meet her at the Belmond."

"In other words, you had been caught."

"That's what I assumed, yes."

"Why did you go?"

"I didn't want to fight in front of Ellie. I knew how Nina could be."

"So she had a history of being volatile?"

"No more than any other woman."

"But we aren't talking about other women, Dr. Hastings. We're talking about your wife. The one you're accused of murdering."

"I didn't kill Nina."

"You were scheduled to leave town the following morning?"

"Yes."

"And you were angry at your wife for putting a deposit down on a group facility home for your daughter?"

"Yes. But—"

"And what happened at the Belmond?"

"I met her in Room 553. She'd reserved it."

"How would you describe her state when you saw her?"

"I told you. I've told everyone. She was dead."

"Yet you didn't call the authorities. You fled."

"I tried to resuscitate her."

"But you just stated that she was deceased when you found her."

"What would you have done? I was in shock. I acted automatically."

"What you also did was destroy a crime scene."

"That's pretty obvious now. But at the time, I wasn't thinking about that."

"What were you thinking about?"

*I was thinking it was my fault; that Nina was in that room because of me.* "I was thinking who would do this…"

"Did you suspect Mrs. Dunaway?"

"No."

"Never?"

"What reason would she have to kill Nina?"

"I don't know. You tell me."

# CHAPTER THIRTY-FOUR

Laurel Dunaway

Journal Entry

It wasn't hard to lie. They made it easy. They set it up so the words could practically roll right off of my tongue. They were convinced they'd caught their killer. They were one step shy of celebrating, a drink or two, pats on the back for a job well done. I was the final step prohibiting them from getting to where they wanted to be. Of course, being the fine officers of the law they are, they were also genuinely curious about what I knew. Even so, they wanted a certain story—an easy story—the kind of story that resulted in the least amount of paperwork. This made it easy to allow them to lead the witness.

"I know this is a shock, Mrs. Dunaway," the detective tells me. He's not sure if he means it. He's sizing me up, trying to gauge what I know. "Forgive me," he says glancing at my statement. "I just want to make sure we have this straight."

I stare at the cold, hard metal table. I've been here before. As a little girl. Not to this police station. But they're pretty much all the same. "Did Mr. Hastings ever give any indication that he might want to kill his wife?" It's *Dr. Hastings,* but I won't bother to correct him. I don't want it to seem like I'm in alliance with the other side. This, and I don't know what Max has told them. I don't know what reasons—if any—they might have for considering my involvement.

"I've offered a written statement," I say, placing one fingertip on the stack of papers. "It's all there."

"I understand," the female detective says. "But sometimes it's good for us to hear it straight from the horse's mouth."

"Sometimes Max scared me. But I didn't think he was capable of murder...." I took a deep breath and looked down at the table. I twist my wedding rings and shake my head. I do not look at either of them. My tears fall against the table. I feel something soft graze my arm. I look up. Tissues.

"No," I say. "I mean, if I'd thought that he'd kill her, I never would have—" I pause and make a point to be careful in my admissions. "I never would have slept with him."

"Did he ever give any indication that he wanted to end things with his wife and take up with you?"

"No. Never."

"Did you assume that might happen? Had you asked him to leave Mrs. Hastings?"

I note the way he says her name, as though he's trying to evoke a reaction out of me. "Our relationship really wasn't like that," I confess, pausing to look genuinely sorry. "I never would have asked Max to do such a thing."

"And why is that?"

"I just didn't feel that way toward him. I'm in love with my husband."

"Yet, you were having an affair," the female detective chimes in.

"Sex and love are not mutually exclusive," I say, and I can tell her counterpart is satisfied. He has all the answers he wants. He does not intend to question me further. She, on the other hand, isn't so sure. "Where were you on the night of Mrs. Hastings's murder?"

"My husband and I attended a dinner party."

"And how did you first hear about Nina Hasting's death?"

"On the news, I suppose. Just like everyone else."

"Were you surprised?"

"I was in shock."

"What did you do after you heard?"

"I spoke with my husband about it."

"So he was aware of the affair?"

"Yes."

"When was the last time you'd spoken with Max Hastings?"

I take some time to think it over. "I can't recall the date. But you have my phone records."

"The affair had been over for several weeks at the time of Mrs. Hastings murder?"

"That's correct."

"What ended it?"

"I did."

"Because your husband confronted you?"

"Yes. And also because my father passed away."

"You were aware that Dr. Hastings had been involved in other adulterous affairs?"

I make sure to look really sullen. "No. Like I said, our relationship wasn't really like that. He was my father's physician. He came on to me. I made a mistake."

"I hear he was quite the Romeo."

I don't respond.

"Does that surprise you?"

"I don't know."

She cocks her head. "You don't know?"

I start crying. Big, fat crocodile tears. "I'm not sure I really knew Max Hastings at all."

"But you just said you didn't love him."

I blow my nose into the sleeve of my shirt. "I didn't. But that doesn't mean it couldn't have just as easily been me that wound up dead," I exclaim, still crying. But I do not implicate Max in the murder. I only state the facts as I know them to be.

"Did Dr. Hastings give you any indication of the sort?"

I tell her about the cat, and the note, and the dead bird on my windshield.

"Did you think he was stalking you?"

"I don't know," I say, and when I don't offer anything more, her partner chimes in. "Max Hastings has confessed to driving by your house on occasion. Late at night."

This is news to me. I place my face in my hands and rub my eyes. "God, how could I have been so stupid?"

There's a collective sigh in the small room. Even two people as jaded as hardened career detectives could imagine a time when they themselves have done really stupid things. My confession is just enough to sway them over to my side. It helps that Max Hastings was an easy target. I guess sometimes you get lucky. I hit the jackpot.

## CHAPTER THIRTY-FIVE

Dr. Max Hastings

AFTER

When you have a body, when that body happens to be *your* wife, when *your* belt is wrapped around your wife's neck, when she is found dead in a hotel room where you frequently take your mistress—what can you expect?

It only goes downhill from there. When every sordid detail of your affair is dragged out for all to see, when the details of your sex life are splashed all over television, the internet, national publications...well, I can say things start to not look very good.

The Belmond doesn't have cameras on the room level or anywhere that matters, apparently. Only in the lobby. Whoever killed Nina did not go out the front entrance. Thankfully, I had Dr. Jones and a very good, very expensive attorney. In the end, the jury handed down a verdict of manslaughter based on criminal negligence. I'll spend ten years in prison. A little more than eight, with good behavior. My defense team did a sufficient job at creating just enough doubt in the juror's minds. Evidence may have been stacked against me, but they couldn't prove that I intentionally went there to kill Nina.

It was suggested that Nina's death was the result of a sex game gone wrong. I know because I'm the one who suggested it.

You see, when you're facing life in prison, you get desperate. I did not see myself coming out of this unscathed. Laurel Dunaway had an alibi for the night of Nina's murder. She and her husband were at a dinner party.

Which meant I got just desperate enough to come up with a good story. I admitted that Nina had found out about the affair. She was distraught. She wanted me to show her what Laurel Dunaway and I were into. In reality, this was not so far-fetched. Most scorned women have a need to hear all of the details. So I confessed. I gave her the details and then I showed her. And that's when things went very, very wrong. I hadn't meant for Nina to die. Which isn't so far from the actual truth.

# CHAPTER THIRTY-SIX

Laurel Dunaway

Journal Entry

The first time came as a surprise. I was well aware of my husband's penchant for hurting women. It's not something he ever hid from me. Hence the club. His aggression, his need for control, his desire to dominate—it's who he is. And when you make a commitment to a person, you commit to loving all of them.

If only he hadn't lied to me. We said from the beginning, whatever happened between us happened. No matter what, we always tell the truth.

We'd both seen enough in our line of work in terms of how lies can destroy lives. We built a business off of lies. A very profitable one, I might add.

The first time was an accident. Even I could see that. The difference between choking a person and suffocating them isn't altogether much. Some are weaker than others, James said. It can be hard to gauge. I'll give him that. With her, it was easy to explain away. The coke in her toxicology report sort of stopped the trail for any real foul play. This, and club members always cover for other members. It goes with it. It's what we do. It adds to the danger. It adds to the allure.

This isn't to say it didn't affect me. The first time a thing happens, you think maybe it's an isolated incident. There's a way to explain it all away. The second time, you take notice. You sense there may be a pattern there. You watch more closely for signs.

The second time was quick. I could see it unraveling. I could see *him* unraveling. James was a shark who'd gotten the taste of blood and was out to find more. Trouble is, what you're seeking often has a way of seeking you.

She showed up late, and equally as important, alone. She took to my husband right away, as most women tend to do. Two weeks later, I learned two things: He'd invited her. And how to dispose of a body. Marriage may be about sacrifice, but I am not one to get my hands dirty. James assured me—he *promised* me—it was the last time. After all, hadn't I seen? She hadn't used the safe word. It was like she wanted to die.

~

THE CAR RIDE FROM THE BELMOND TO THE PARTY WAS A TENSE ONE. "How did you know?" he asked, with false calm. The tautness in his jaw and the crease between his brows easily gave him away.

"You were chatting with her *on our app*. Chats I moderate. A better question would be...*how* did you *not* think I would find out?" I said. Nina Hastings was a lie in more ways than one. She was different. She was a sign. My husband wasn't going to stop. He was introducing a new level to an old game. He was testing more than my patience. He was testing my love.

"Why didn't you say anything?"

*Because it was apparent right away you were fucking her.* "What good would it have done? It had already happened."

"Jesus, Laurel. A normal wife would have said something. Until the incident at the office, you never even let on. And even then, it wasn't about the affair, was it?"

I heard the question behind the question. *Is it because of him? Do you have feelings for him?* James hadn't asked for an open marriage, but he was, in his own way, showing me he wanted one.

"You lied to me. What did you expect?"

"Well, I'll tell you what I didn't expect," he told me, his voice full of edge. "I didn't expect you to go and start fucking Max Hastings."

I didn't say anything. Not for a long while. I was thinking about Nina, about her lifeless body lying on the bed where her husband and I once had so much pleasure. I was thinking of her vacant stare and wondering why she hadn't known better. I was thinking that maybe James is right; maybe I should have confronted him sooner. But where's the honor in that?

A stoplight up ahead flashed yellow. He slammed on the brakes even though he had plenty of time to come to a full stop. "Laurel. Answer me."

"Because I knew, okay? I knew this wouldn't end well," I said. He'd made that painfully obvious when he invited her to the club and then to work for us. No one can prepare you for what it's like.

Dr. Miller talks about grief. Well, nothing could have prepared me for what it would be like to sit back and watch the person you love fall in love with someone who isn't you. But that's what I did. "Because I knew that eventually it had to end. And because you're the one always talking about the importance of having an exit strategy."

"Is that what he is to you? Your exit strategy?"

"No," I replied, earnestly. "He was my safety net."

"Gun to your head?"

I swallowed hard. "Gun to my head, that's the only reason I seduced him."

It wasn't a lie. I knew James would eventually take things too far. He didn't really love her—he was merely upping the stakes, making the game more enticing. Nina Hastings was not the first woman my husband killed intentionally. But with any luck, she will be the last.

$\sim$

"Something doesn't add up for me, Laurel..." James says, pulling me into a spare bedroom. I see it; even in the dim light, I see it. That fire, it's there in his eyes.

"Come on," I said. "We have to get back to the party. We have to be *seen*. You know what's at stake."

He sucked in a hard breath and then let it out. "We will. But first, you owe me an explanation."

My eyes scanned the room. There was a table lamp, and a desk chair, but not much else that could serve as a weapon. I've seen my husband kill more than one woman, and I don't for a second doubt that I may be next. My heart leaped so high into my throat that I could have easily opened my mouth and touched it. I glanced wildly back at him, jerking my neck in the process. If there was ever a time to employ false bravado, this was it. "What, James?" I hissed. "What is so goddamned impor-tant that you're putting our freedom—our pleasure—on the line?"

He looked serenely at me, head slightly lowered in what I took for curiosity, as though he were seeing me for the first time. What I saw reflected back to me was a gift, something offered with a carelessness that was appealing. "It just doesn't add up. That bull-shit story you fed me. It's too neat—too pretty. I started fucking Nina Hastings...and you...you just happened to "run into" her husband?"

*God, you're such an idiot, James.* "Of course not. I had to have a reason."

His expression told me he didn't follow.

"It's a long story…"

"We have time." He took my hand and led me to the bed. "Tell me every little thing," he said, and so I did.

I tell him that it didn't hurt that Max was an easy target. The method might have been a little extreme. Thankfully, I've never lacked imagination. When I initially discovered that my husband had been chatting with a woman on Beacon, I did my research. I found out her name, where she worked, who she was married to. Anything you can imagine, it was at my fingertips. Most of it she'd offered up herself in conversation with my husband.

THERE ARE A LOT OF THINGS I WITHHOLD FROM JAMES. SOMETIMES you skim the surface with the truth and hope that it suffices. Once news of Nina's murder broke, it sort of had to. We were busy: Busy doing damage control. Busy seducing the press and the police. I learned a lot over the course of those months. I hope my husband did too.

Lesson one: Don't ask. Don't tell. First, I went to the hospital. I volunteered. This took a total of sixteen hours of my time. More than I would have liked, but the end result was worth it, so who's to say whether it was worth it? With my husband busy seducing another woman, it's not like I didn't have extra time on my hands.

It was easy, really. I chatted up the other volunteers, along with a few of the nurses. This isn't a direct lesson, just a side note: Pretending you have an interest in someone you don't can take you a long way. People love to talk about themselves. They can't help it. Which is how eventually the staff told me what I needed to know. They told me which patients had family, and they told me about the sad cases, those that didn't. "Dad" turned out to be one of those. I began volunteering to sit with him, and when the time came for him to be discharged, you'd better believe I planted the notion of Caring Hands in his damaged brain. He had dementia. It wasn't hard. How else was I supposed to get close to Max Hastings in a way that wouldn't leave him suspicious? In a way that would get under his skin. I learned Max's history. His likes and dislikes. Hell, I even learned how and when he lost his virginity. Then I took it a step further. I inserted myself into the story. If it hadn't been that one, it would have been another. It's only important that it be significant. It was easy to insert myself into Max's life, to pretend we had history, because all he could think about was fucking me. My fake dad didn't—or rather *couldn't*— argue about it not being true. Therefore the rule of familiarity allowed me to enter his life and plot my scheme.

My husband never questioned me on any of it. Why? Because my husband isn't the only one good at keeping secrets. He doesn't really know me; he only knows what I've told him. When my sick father made a sudden reappearance in my life, he didn't think to question any of it because I'd only ever fed him what I wanted him to know.

Lesson two: history always repeats itself. My husband has a history of finding himself with dead women on his hands. That meant I had to be prepared. Lesson two, part two: befriend the fall guy. Just in case.

The truth is, I never expected to like Max Hastings. But I did. His wife—the one who was fucking my husband, infiltrating my business, and my life—well, she was another story. I knew I had to be patient. So I endured Max's stupid, methodical, misogynistic sex games over the course of all of those months. I never complained. Not even once.

Lesson three: nothing is free. All relationships are transactional in nature. Max thought he could take what he wanted from me and give little in return. He never cared to have a future with me. He never even thought about it. I know because I asked. He was willing to take what he could get, because I was willing to give it. All of that aggression...did he not understand that like attracts like? Did he not think that I might be harboring a little rage of my own? And did he not think that it might be turned around and be redirected right back at him?

There's a saying about casualties of war—that's what Max was. He married a woman who tried to take something that wasn't hers to take. Granted, my husband was probably just going to kill her, if I didn't beat him to the punch. And if I had been wrong, if he really had loved her? What then? With our business about to sell, with so much at stake, I couldn't take any chances. We needed a quick resolution. Max was the catalyst to that. He was the fuel that ignited the fire. I only had to get close to him, come up with a story that suggested he was capable of murder, which happened inadvertently in my deposition when I explained Max's role in my fake father's care. Of course, I mentioned that we had discussed physician-assisted suicide. But we weren't serious about it. At least I wasn't. And, of course he had thought it would help to double-dose my father's pain medication prior to his death. Max said he wanted me to get some rest. He said, that way, we would all get some rest.

Oh, and those bite marks? They were kindling. I knew James would find out eventually. I'd hoped she'd be the one to tell him. I mean... how else was she going to disappear? Everyone knows it's always the husband.

Thankfully, people are often wrong. I was lucky. The press assumed a man loved me enough to kill for me. They were right in that sense—just not entirely. In the end, only three people really know what happened in Room 553. Max Hastings, it turned out, wasn't one of them.

# CHAPTER THIRTY-SEVEN

Laurel Dunaway

Journal Entry

The little girl's real father died in a boating accident, but not the way most people think. For years, he would come into the little girl's room to seek comfort—and not the way daddies are supposed to. Maybe this was why the mommy did what she did all those years ago. Maybe she was trying to save the girl and herself too. Maybe some secrets are too big to hold onto. Maybe you have to bury them before they bury you.

Maybe the little girl had to learn this for herself.

∼

I VISITED MAX'S DAUGHTER TODAY AT HER NEW SCHOOL. IT WASN'T an easy endeavor, by any stretch of the imagination. But as they say, where there's a will there's a way.

It's a shame that Nina ended up getting what she wanted in the manner she did. I remember how down Max looked when he mentioned it. I don't have many regrets, but the fact that I hadn't offered him more in that moment is one of them.

I think he'd be glad to know it's a good place. My visit was short, but I told her that her dad had sent me and that he wanted her to know he loved her very much. I told her he would be coming to get her just as soon as he could. I don't know if that's true; Max and I haven't spoken, but it was the least I could do. She cocked her head and blinked her eyes. I don't know if she heard me. She only said, "Promise." I'd like to think that she understood.

# CHAPTER THIRTY-EIGHT

Laurel Dunaway

Journal Entry

T he first thoughts to properly stick were about the timing. Specifically, had it been enough? Could I get away with it? Could I be really and truly free? The second was the taste of bile rising in my throat. I could feel it. *This is it.* Finally, my life was really and truly about to begin again.

He's going to die, and there's nothing I can do to stop it. *This is where it ends.* James would brush it off, if I were to tell him how truly terrifying this all felt. If I were to tell him— which I can't— he would tell me I was overacting. But then, how could he know that? It's hard to say until you get to the end, and we weren't there yet.

In my mind, it wasn't an exaggeration. It was real. It's always real. I picture his funeral. I imagine his casket, me draping myself over it, acting like a proper widow. A monument to a man I once really loved. *God, please make it quick.*

The mind works in mysterious ways under extreme duress. In the haze of being woken from sleep, the pieces of the puzzle rarely fit. It's always the same, and yet, it never is. My heart races. The back of my neck feels clammy. The sickly feeling, deep down in the pit of my stomach, made itself known. Even though I've been waiting for precisely this moment, I still have all the normal reactions. Some things you just can't shake.

Just ask my husband. Not that you can, because he's dead asleep.

The alarm chimed persistently, growing louder and louder by the second, reminding me this is reality. This is happening. *Finally.* Even in the thick of sleep, I am keenly aware this isn't the normal alarm. It is *the* alarm. The one I've been waiting for, for the past fourteen months.

Rubbing my eyes, I checked his Dexcom monitor. Three characters told me everything I needed to know, which wasn't much. But enough. The situation was dire. There wasn't even a numerical reading. It just read: *low.* Thank the Lord.

I lurched out of bed, picking up pace as I half-stumbled down the hall, slowing only when I got to the stairs, then power-walking as I rounded the corner into the kitchen. I opened the fridge, grabbed one of the two-dozen bottles of orange juice we keep on hand precisely for this kind of situation.

I wiped my sweaty, shaky hands on a dishrag, took a deep breath, and then deftly twisted the cap off the juice. I grabbed a straw from the drawer, flung it in, and took a seat on the sofa. I checked the time. Two forty-seven in the morning. I don't know how long these things take, but it's safe to say my husband will probably be dead by sunrise. God willing.

It was unfortunate that this couldn't have happened a little later, so that at least I could have gotten my eight hours in. It would be nice if I could just fall back to sleep, but I'm too wired. It helped, certainly, that my mind had already lurched into the future, ticking off items on my to-do list. *It's Friday. A tennis lesson. A massage. Dinner with friends. No. Wait. That's wrong. It's not Friday. As usual, I'm ahead of myself. Today is Thursday...A derm appointment. Botox...that's it. After that, my schedule is free and clear.*

Not that it mattered. No matter what was on the agenda, I'd be exhausted. Another thought flittered in and then out. *It'll help you sell the story.* With any luck, I could very well be spending the afternoon making funeral arrangements. I shook my head. It's better not to count your chickens before they hatch. I maintain a vise-like grip on the cold juice as I suck it down. Then I flip on the TV and I wait.

# EPILOGUE

Max Hastings

Twelve Years Later

We have a saying in Texas: big hat, no cattle. It's about appearing one way but being another. There's another I'm quite fond of as well: never trade what you want most for what you want now at the moment. If only it were a lesson I'd learned sooner. It took me a long time to work out *if* and *why* Laurel would have killed Nina. I couldn't see a motive. I suppose my own guilt about the affair, and in getting my wife mixed up in it, came to play.

In the end, I had been looking at it all wrong.

The truth unraveled slowly, as truth tends to do. Shortly after my sentencing, a donation came through. Initially, following my arrest, my brother had taken Ellie in. But when it became obvious that my stay was not going to be a relatively short one, Nina posthumously got her way. I signed papers for my daughter to be placed in a care facility. Jonathan was not equipped to raise a child, particularly not one with Ellie's circumstances. My brother took out a second mortgage on his house to cover it. The sale of mine had paid for my defense. Almost.

It wasn't a spectacular care facility; I could assimilate that, given the price. My brother's expression when we spoke about it provided verification that my assumptions were correct. If I hadn't slept well in jail, prison—combined with the situation with my daughter—elevated that ten-fold. Anyhow, when the anonymous donation came in, it came with a note about a facility. Ellie was moved two weeks later. Had things not have unfolded the way they had, I may have never truly been able to say for sure that Laurel Dunaway killed my wife. Experience has taught me that guilt is a powerful motivator. It tends to bring things to light.

I'm not sure whether it was guilt or if Laurel was simply toying with me, rubbing her freedom and my lack thereof in my face. It's hard to say when you realize a person you thought you knew is not someone you ever really knew at all.

Not long after Ellie was moved, I learned about the sale of the Dunaways business. Jonathan never offered me much in the way of Laurel Dunaway, just bits and pieces here and there. He didn't think it was healthy to speak of her. On many occasions, he accused me of being obsessed. And more than once, I saw the look in his eyes, one that said he wondered if I actually had killed Nina.

Three years into my prison sentence, by way of an obituary, I learned of the death of James Dunaway. It was written that he went into a diabetic coma and passed away eight days later, a victim of his disease. I was both surprised and not.

I WAS RELEASED FROM PRISON ON A WEDNESDAY. LAUREL DUNAWAY would be found hanging from the stairwell of her home the following Friday. One good thing, and maybe the only good thing about prison, is that it affords you the opportunity to see a variety of "suicides," so you get to know which ones work and which ones lead to tacked on sentences.

I would like to say that she was surprised to see me standing at her bedside in the dark. But I don't think she was. I selected the same manner of death that she had chosen for my wife. *An eye for an eye makes the whole world blind,* she said.

*I was once blind but now I see,* I had replied. That made her smile.

I would also like to say that I felt nothing during the process. Dying is, after all, a process, but that would be untrue. Laurel Dunaway was the same, all those years later, that she had been the day I first laid eyes on her. Charming, seductive. Cunning. Helpless. Someone looking to be saved.

Although, she could not be saved in the end. None of us could.

Police did their due diligence, which is how Laurel's journal was discovered. It turned out there was a lot about the Dunaways' that folks didn't know. No doubt Laurel wanted it this way. She liked the limelight just as much as she understood she had to hide from it.

Twenty-six months later, I would provide testimony in front of the senate about false confessions and botched evidence. Two months after that, I would receive a settlement from the state. The money doesn't negate what happened to me. It will never buy me back all the years I lost. But I try not to think too much about that.

These days, my daughter and I live in an undisclosed location. I do not date much.

# A NOTE FROM BRITNEY

Dear Reader,

I hope you enjoyed reading *ROOM 553*.

Writing a book is an interesting adventure, it's a bit like inviting people into your brain to rummage around. *Look where my imagination took me. These are the kind of stories I like...*

That feeling is often intense and unforgettable. And mostly, a ton of fun.

With that in mind—thank you again for reading my work. I don't have the backing or the advertising dollars of big publishing, but hopefully I have something better... readers who like the same kind of stories I do. If you are one of them, please share with your friends and consider helping out by doing one (or all) of these quick things:

1. Visit my review page and write a 30 second review (even short ones make a big difference).

**(http://britneyking.com/aint-too-proud-to-beg-for-reviews/)**

Many readers don't realize what a difference reviews make but they make ALL the difference.

2. Drop me an email and let me know you left a review. This way I can enter you into my monthly drawing for signed paperback copies.

**(hello@britneyking.com)**

3. Point your psychological thriller loving friends to their free copies of my work. My favorite friends are those who introduce me to books I might like. **(http://www.britneyking.com)**

4. If you'd like to make sure you don't miss anything, to receive an email whenever I release a new title, sign up for my new release newsletter.

**(https://britneyking.com/new-release-alerts/)**

Thanks for helping, and for reading my work. It means a lot.

Britney King

Austin, Texas

June 2019

# ABOUT THE AUTHOR

Britney King lives in Austin, Texas with her husband, children, two dogs, one ridiculous cat, and a partridge in a peach tree.

When she's not wrangling the things mentioned above, she writes psychological, domestic and romantic thrillers set in suburbia.

Without a doubt, she thinks connecting with readers is the best part of this gig. You can find Britney online here:

**Email:** britney@britneyking.com
**Web:** https://britneyking.com
**Facebook:** https://www.facebook.com/BritneyKingAuthor
**Instagram:** https://www.instagram.com/britneyking_/
**Twitter:** https://twitter.com/BritneyKing_
**Goodreads:** https://bit.ly/BritneyKingGoodreads
**Pinterest:** https://www.pinterest.com/britneyking_/

Happy reading.

*Breaking Bedrock* / Book Two

*Beyond Bedrock* / Book Three

*The Bedrock Series Box Set*

The Bedrock Series features an unlikely heroine who should have known better. Turns out, she didn't. Thus she finds herself tangled in a messy, dangerous, forbidden love story and face-to-face with a madman hell-bent on revenge. The series has been compared to Fatal Attraction, Single White Female, and Basic Instinct.

*Around The Bend*

Around The Bend, is a heart-pounding standalone which traces the journey of a well-to-do suburban housewife, and her life as it unravels, thanks to the secrets she keeps. If she were the only one with things she wanted to keep hidden, then maybe it wouldn't have turned out so bad. But she wasn't.

*Somewhere With You* / Book One

*Anywhere With You* / Book Two

*The With You Series Box Set*

The With You Series at its core is a deep love story about unlikely friends who travel the world; trying to find themselves, together and apart. Packed with drama and adventure along with a heavy dose of suspense, it has been compared to The Secret Life of Walter Mitty and Love, Rosie.

## ACKNOWLEDGMENTS

Many thanks to my family and friends. I appreciate the endless inspiration. But most of all that you put up with my creative process. No easy feat, I know.

Thank you to the beta team, ARC team, and the book bloggers. You make this gig so fun. I wouldn't want to do it without you. Your part is more essential to the equation than you know.

Last, but certainly not least, many thanks to you for reading my work. I appreciate you making this dream of mine come true.

# SNEAK PEEK: WATER UNDER THE BRIDGE

## BOOK ONE

**In the spirit of *Gone Girl* and *Behind Closed Doors* comes a gripping, twisting, furiously clever read that demands your attention, and keeps you guessing until the very end. For fans of the anti-heroine and stories told in unorthodox ways, *Water Under The Bridge* delivers us the perfect dark and provocative villain.**

As a woman who feels her clock ticking every single moment of the day, former bad girl Kate Anderson is desperate to reinvent herself. So when she sees a handsome stranger walking toward her, she feels it in her bones, there's no time like the present. *He's the one.*

Kate vows to do whatever it takes to have what she wants, even if that something is becoming someone else. Now, ten pounds thinner, armed with a new name, and a plan, she's this close to living the perfect life she's created in her mind.

*But Kate has secrets.*

And too bad for her, that handsome stranger has a few of his own.

With twists and turns you won't see coming, Water Under The Bridge examines the pressure that many women feel to "have it all" and introduces a protagonist whose hard edges and cutthroat ambition will leave you questioning your judgment and straddling the line between what's right and wrong.

**Enjoy dark fiction? Are you a fan of stories told in unique ways? If so, you'll love Britney King's bestselling psychological thrillers. Get to know Jude and Kate, unreliable narrators at best, intense, and, in your face at worst.** *Water Under The Bridge* **is the first book in The Water Trilogy. Available in digital and print.**

*DEAD IN THE WATER* **(Book Two) and** *COME HELL OR HIGH WATER* **(Book Three) are now available.**

<u>**What readers are saying:**</u>

*"Another amazingly well-written novel by Britney King. It's every bit as dark, twisted and mind twisting as Water Under The Bridge...maybe even a little more so."*

*"Hands down- best book by Britney King. Yet. She has delivered a difficult writing style so perfectly and effortlessly, that you just want to worship the book for the writing. The author has managed to make murder/assassination/accidental- gunshot- to-the-head- look easy. Necessary."*

*"Having fallen completely head over heels for these characters and this author with the first book in the series, I've been pretty much salivating over the thought of this book for months now. You'll be glad to know that it did not disappoint!"*

<u>**Series Praise**</u>

*"If Tarantino were a woman and wrote novels... they might read a bit like this."*

*"Fans of Gillian Flynn and Paula Hawkins meet your next obsession."*

*"Provocative and scary."*

*"A dark and edgy page-turner. What every good thriller is made of."*

*"I devoured this novel in a single sitting, absolutely enthralled by the storyline. The suspense was clever and unrelenting!"*

*"Completely original and complex."*

*"Compulsive and fun."*

*"No-holds-barred villains. Fine storytelling full of mystery and suspense."*

*"Fresh and breathtaking insight into the darkest corners of the human psyche."*

# HER

BRITNEY KING

# COPYRIGHT

HER is a work of fiction. Names, characters, places, images, and incidents are products of the author's imagination or are used fictitiously and are not to be construed as real. Any resemblance to actual events, locales, organizations, persons, living or dead, is entirely coincidental and not intended by the author. The scanning, uploading, and distribution of this book without permission is a theft of the author's intellectual property. No part of this publication may be used, shared or reproduced in any manner whatsoever without written permission except in the case of brief quotations embodied in critical articles and reviews. If you would like permission to use material from the book (other than for review purposes), please contact http://britneyking.com/contact/ Thank you for your support of the author's rights.

Hot Banana Press
Cover Design by Britney King LLC
Cover Image by Britney King LLC
Copy Editing by Librum Artis Editorial Service
Proofread by Proofreading by the Page

Copyright © 2019 by Britney King LLC. All Rights Reserved.

First Edition: 2019
ISBN 13: 978-1797040912
ISBN 10: 1797040912

britneyking.com

*This is not for you.*

"The truth will set you free, but first it will piss you off." — Joe Klaas

# PROLOGUE

## *Now*

I wish someone had told me: worry is a waste of time. The real troubles of your life will be things that never even bothered to cross your mind.

Nine months, three days, and nineteen hours, I've lived down the street from her. If you really think about it, a person can do a lot in nine months. They can gestate a fetus and deliver it safely into the world, and they can also plant roots and create an entirely different life altogether. That's what she did.

Not that I realized it at the time, but in essence, that's what she helped me to do, too. What's good for the goose is good for the gander, as they say. Only she isn't a bird. She can't just fly away, the way she thinks she can.

She thinks she can migrate, start a new life elsewhere, someplace where she can be whatever she wants to be. But she's forgetting two things: wherever you go, there you are. Also, there are people like me.

When I moved to this boring, homogeneous, monotonous

little town, I did so with one intention and one intention only: to have a nice life. A quiet life.

That's not how it played out. Not even close.

First, it was good. And then it got bad before it got good again.

I met her and life changed.

What can I say? I got swept up in it. She makes it easy. Her, with her impractical shoes and her perpetually sunny nature. For me, she always has felt a bit like spring in the middle of winter. She was then, and still is to me now, just about the most wonderful thing in the world.

But there's something to be said for that. Something I hadn't realized at the start. It was a new experience for me, and I felt dizzy for a while. Like most things, dizziness fades. And then, it dawns on you, the relationship you have in your mind is profoundly different from the one you actually have.

Of course, it takes precious time before you figure this out. Only by then, it's too late. By then, desire has already taken you to the darkest edges of humanity. It's a special place in the deepest recesses of hell, let me tell you. That's when you realize what they say is true: Every love affair has its rituals—and you always kill what you love in the end.

On so many occasions, this could have taken a different route. She could have proven me wrong, and yet so many times she took exactly the route I predicted. We all make choices. She made hers. I made mine. Those choices have consequences. I'd like to think I've been lenient with her, far more lenient than I should have been.

So, that's how I've found myself here, at the end that's really a beginning. Here, in her kitchen, sitting at her bar, turning the knife over in my hands. All the while knowing that what awaits me upstairs will not be easy.

It's okay.

No one ever said revenge was easy. Just sweet. One of her favorite sayings. She was wrong about a lot of things—me, for one

—but *that*, well, that she was right about. Revenge is surprisingly sweet. It's clear in the steadiness of my breath, in the clarity that has washed over me. My hands don't even shake.

There are eleven steps to the top of the stairs. I've counted.

Her death will not be random. A crime of passion, they'll call it. Although it will not be done in the heat of the moment, the way one might suspect. No. This is a scene I've played out in my mind, hundreds, if not thousands, of times. I knew it wouldn't be easy. She is my friend, my only friend. She prefers it that way.

Yes, I am aware of how pathetic this sounds. I wish I knew how to make you understand. It's just…well, I've never been very good with words. That's her gift. Mine is asking questions. Maybe I should start there. Have you ever met someone you know is absolutely terrible for you but for whatever reason, combined with all the mysteries of the universe, you just can't help yourself? Well, for me, that person is her.

I can't help myself. She's black magic and at the same time the air I need to breathe. Which is why I was careful to prepare for any and all setbacks. Setbacks have always been our specialty.

I finish off my Danish, careful to savor it in the way that she would appreciate. Next, I slip off my shoes, and leave them neatly by the door, just as I have countless times before, on more pleasant visits.

To outsiders, her death will come as a shock. Obviously, not for long. I've accounted for this. Which is to say, I don't plan to stick around. Statistics show most victims know their perpetrators. Murder is astonishingly predictable. Since the beginning of time we've been sleeping, eating, having sex, and murdering each other. And not necessarily in that order.

Why no one ever sees these things coming is beyond me.

She really should have seen it coming.

Trust is a slippery thing though, isn't it? Intangible, I've come to find. It doesn't matter how smart your brain is. The heart is a different organ entirely. At least, this is the only logical explanation I can come up with as to why the truth so often remains elusive even when it's dangled right in front of us. It isn't logical at all. For so long, I thought if I just tried hard enough, I could make this work. There's a price for that kind of stupidity. And believe me, I paid it.

Now, it's her turn.

You live and you learn, I suppose. And let me tell you, I have learned…

At the top of the stairs, I will find her in her bed, third door to the right. By this time of night, she will be sleeping on her side, covers pulled halfway up. Her expression will be slack, but peaceful, for even in sleep women like her know only ease.

On the left side of the four-poster bed, is a nightstand. On top of the nightstand rests her Bible, the cell phone she'll never reach, a glass of water she'll never drink, the reading glasses she doesn't want anyone to know she needs.

I will attack from the right, stabbing her six times. I've mapped it out. Six stab wounds, one for each of the ways she has wronged me. In reality, it doesn't take that much to kill a person. She probably knows this better than anyone. And if not, just in case, I want to make sure.

Made in the USA
Monee, IL
27 November 2021